Romance Suspense

Dear Reader,

It has been an absolute joy writing this book. Words can only express the wonderful world that sometimes appears in my head. Bringing this story to life was nothing less than exciting and fulfilling. Riding this rollercoaster of events and emotions has been incredible. Restoration is available for all and this book puts that in words

The friends and loved ones who have been an encouragement to me while completing this work mean the world to me. Special thanks to a few close friends who helped to develop this work into what it has become. Your contributions will no be forgotten.

Enjoy this romance ride and cling to your seats during the turbulence. Thanks for being the greatest audience of readers in the world.

Ronnie L. Lee

MISTAKES

Ronnie L. Lee

ISBN – 978-0-692-91166-2

MISTAKES

Copyright @ 2017 by Ronnie L. Lee

This is a work of **FICTION**. Names, characters, places and incidents are either the production of the author's imagination or are used fictitiously, and any

For questions and comments about the quality of this book please contact us on facebook @ Mistakes the Suspense

Printed in U.S.A

MISTAKES

Ronnie L. Lee

CHAPTER 1

Late afternoon at the close of a busy workday, Sandra and her boyfriend cap off the night making passionate love. Her bedroom is lit only by, the candle on the neatly arranged dresser. Twenty seven year old Adam's busy work schedule has made it almost impossible to spend any consistent time together with Sandra. Sandra is preparing dinner for what she hopes will be the perfect night. Adam's clean-cut appearance and athletic frame has Sandra really hoping and praying that this relationship will be unlike her past short-lived ones. The wine is chilled and the salad is tossed. The table is set and the aroma of seared steak saturates the air.

They meet at the door. Sandra is dressed very sexy leaving little to Adam's imagination. His attention is quickly arrested by the sweet smell of her perfume.

"Wow, now this is what I call the ideal greeting. Hey, I got a great idea; let's save dinner for later and enjoy the appetizer in the bedroom first?"

Sandra smiled. Adam dropped his jacket on the sofa and the two made their way down the hallway to the bedroom. The noises of passion resonated throughout the apartment. There sexual needs are meticulously and sufficiently met.

"Sandra, I could really get used to this special attention. Can we make a date tomorrow for round two?"

"That sounds like a wonderful plan honey." Sandra placed her hand over her mouth to hide the joy she felt as she went to warm up the dinner.

As the night grew late Adam says, "I really, really had a wonderful time. I don't know if I'm going to be able to work tomorrow just thinking about round two."

'Ok' She replied, "I'll make sure I wear something even more sexier."

"Hey, less is good too."

"You are too funny. Goodnight."

"Good night, Sandra."

If you keep hugging me like this I don't think I'm going to be able to leave. The two made plans to talk the next day. As he left she leaned on the doorframe. She smiled and said, "I think he might be the perfect guy for me!"

CHAPTER 2

The glare of the sun lights the landscape of Chestnut in the city of Buffalo, New York. It was early in the morning, the neatly manicured grass, dripping wet by the constant clicks of the water sprinklers irrigating in anticipation of a seasonably hot and humid summer day. In the middle of this residential block, a two story white frame home sat with drawn draperies. Around the back of the asphalt driveway the kitchen sits with windows overlooking Jennifer's mini-van parked next to her husband Steve's, black BMW with slightly tented windows.

The grinding sound of Jennifer's blender loaded with fresh fruits, melons and strawberries for her routine morning smoothie followed up her early morning jog. On his way down the carpeted stairs, Steve's trot came to a pause at the bottom step.

"Wow! Honey, you can't add to excellence. The way those jogging pants are hitting your hips is nothing less than a picture of flawless perfection."

Jennifer responds, "Oh really?"

"You know, maybe we should head back upstairs so you can work off some of that early-morning energy you've built up?"

She responded, "Well, what about work?"

"The look of your shape is having an effect on me." Steve stepped around the counter and rubbed his body up against Jennifer's buttock and slowly kissed her on the back of her neck. "What do you say, sexy?"

"You know sometimes I think that sex is the only thing you men ever think about."

"But, that's a good thing don't you think? Not to mention, it has been quite a while since we made love Jennifer."

"Oh Steve, so now you're keeping score?" Jennifer reached over to get a paper towel.

"I'll take that as a no to my love making offer?"

Steve grabbed his brown bag lunch off the counter, picks up his brief case, and slowly headed for the locked back door. Okay then, "How about we spend some personal, quiet time in the bedroom tonight?"

Peering over the rim of her smoothie, "Personal time, really, Steve?"

He responded, "Yes, personal time. What do you have going on after work today if you don't mind me asking?

Jennifer slammed her glass down on the counter; "What, now are you checking up on me?" Aren't you going to be late for work or something?"

"No, Ms. Smarty. I was hoping we could finally spend time together."

"Not today, my friend Kelly moved into her new place and, after work I'm going over to help her unpack and get settled in."

"But, I was talking about us unpacking each other and; me settling in with you, hint, hint, hint?" He winked.

"No dammit, I promised and she's expecting me!"

"Well, dammit. Why am I always the one being neglected?"

"Steve, why don't you just have another drink; lately that seems to be working wonders for you?"

Hell, "There's nothing wrong with a couple of beers after work. Maybe I'm drinking more because I keep getting less, know what I mean wifey?"

"Well, if you can't wait then do what you men do to take care of yourselves." She shrugged. "And, stop trying to send me on a guilt trip because you can't control your hyperactive libido!"

"Wow, I didn't know that this would cause you to become so defensive and upset."

Jennifer disassembled the blender and washed it. "In case you didn't know it, life is bigger than your ever-increasing sex drive. There are more important things going on in my world besides satisfying your sexual demands!"

Steve adjusted the collar on his suit jacket, "Well, you have a nice day too, Jennifer." Her phone rang, "Oh, and before you answer that Damn phone, which seems to get much more attention than me these days, it's reassuring to know that your husband's needs are not important to you at all!"

Steve slammed the screen door and stomped down the stairs. Steve's rear tires screeched as he sped off.

CHAPTER 3

Arriving to work at the CDI Engineering Firm building, Steve yelled, "What the hell! Someone is parked in my spot again." He hurried out of his car and onto the elevator, headed for the twelfth floor.

"This day is really starting off with a bang, I wonder what will the rest of it bring." On the twelfth floor Steve walked past the receptionist, Tammy, "Good morning."

In his office Steve dropped his briefcase, hangs up his jacket, and sat at his desk. As usual Tammy placed a fresh cup of coffee on his desk made just the way Steve likes it, easy cream, two sugars, and a shot of caramel mocha.

The noise of the office workers is matched only by, the footsteps of the hallway traffic, as employees carry on their business. Steve glanced at the photo of him and Jennifer that sat on his desk. He called Jennifer. "Damn a busy signal. I hope she's not ignoring the phone call."

Speaking through a half open door Steve asked, "Tammy can you check to see if those figures came in for the proposal?"

"One minute, Sir, I'll check."

Steve turned his chair toward the window taking in the sunlight and the architectural landscape of the surrounding building. "Excuse me, Sir. No, the numbers for the proposal are not in yet."

"Tammy, I need you to call *ASAP* and see what the holdup is! I desperately need those proposal numbers."

A knock came at the door. "Yes Tammy."

"Sir, you have a visitor."

"Okay, send them in."

Dressed in cargo slacks and a blue sports jacket a process server displays for Steve his ID and hands Steve a business card. "Are you Steve Mc. Dermott?"

"I am. What's this about?"

"In that case, these documents are for you." He hands Steve a packet of paper with the words stamped on it in bold print **DISSOLUTION OF MARRIAGE**. "Have a nice day!"

"Somehow I knew this damn day wasn't going to get any better."

"What the hell, I can't believe this, how dare she do this to me!" Steve grabs the envelope and rips it open. He tries Jennifer's number again. "Irreconcilable differences; you got to be kidding!"

"Hello, Jennifer, how the hell could you do this to me? A divorce! Why didn't you talk to me about this before you went this far? After all we've been through over the last three years? Listen, you've got to rethink this!"

"Steve I've given this too much thought and I've made up my mind to end this now and move on with my life. I've had enough. I'm moving out and I'll pick up the rest of my things later."

"Move on with your life, moving on to what?"

"Jennifer, come on, Honey, lets slow down and think this over. Let me try to make things right?"

"Steve, I want to be truthful with you because, despite your drinking issues, you're a really good guy, "

"Come on, honey, l know things have been a bit rough but I promise you we can make this marriage work. I love you, let's get some counseling; talk to the Pastor or something!"

"Steve, listen."

"Jennifer, please don't do this."

"Steve, please listen. I've got to tell you something else."

"What else, hell, you've already said more than enough!"

"I'm deeply in love with Kelly and we're getting married. We plan to spend the rest of our lives together."

Steve replied, "Oh my God, honey, please tell me you're joking. Is this some sort of prank?"

"Steve, I'm not joking. That was always your problem, you never took me serious."

"You know, I thought there was something strange about that friendship. What about our vows? What about starting a family, Listen Jen, it's probably just a phase, we can work through that too."

Jennifer shouted. "It's not a phase! It's over! The matter is no longer open for discussion!" Jennifer slammed the phone down!

After a quick tap on the door Steve's boss peered in. "Steve, I need that proposal on my desk by 1:00 o'clock pm. You're not making things any easier around here, everyone's got to bare their own load in this office."

Steve looked at the picture of he and his wife and, lowered his head in his hands. Steve angrily placed another call to Jennifer who answered. "Steve, I've made my decision; it's over! Please don't call me anymore!" Steve begins yelling and Jennifer ends the call.

At one o'clock Steve sat in his office and Tammy walked in. "Steve the Proposal figures have not arrived reason being, I inadvertently gave the carrier the wrong address for delivery."

"Oh my God Mr. Scott is going to lose it!"

Just then Mr. Scott walked in. "Steve, where is the proposal? I've got to send it off before the post office closes?

"Sir, I don't have it yet; I need another day."

"Dammit, Steve, this is unacceptable! I suggest that you get your act together or you'll be looking for another job in the very near future." Steve plopped down at his desk as his boss stormed out.

As the workday comes to a close Steve tells Tammy, "Tammy, we've got to be on top of that proposal first thing in the morning, I truly can't handle any more stress. After a day like this I need a drink. Well, maybe I should just turn in early? On second thought, I need a stiff drink to help me deal with all of the drama. I'll just stop for a few minutes and then go home. Maybe by then Jennifer will have came to her senses."

CHAPTER 4

At the corner of Walden and Genesee is the neighborhood bar, The Golden Ladle. Steve expected to have a tranquil moment with good music and a few beers.

Steve took a seat on the stool at the end of the bar. "Bartender, I'll have a beer. It's been a very strenuous day and I just want to relax a while before going home."

After throwing down a few bottles of beer, Steve took his half-full beer over to an empty table off in the corner of the bar. He thought, out of sight and out of mind.

Julie, a regular at the bar, caught Steve's gazes as she danced to the rhythmic sounds of Kanye West and Jamie Foxx; Gold Digger playing in the background. "She take my money when I'm in need, yeah she's a trifling friend indeed. Oh she's a gold digger way over town that digs on me. (She gives me money). Now I ain't sayin' she a gold digger; (when I'm in need). But she ain't messin' with no broke da broke. (She gives me money). Now I ain't sayin' she a gold digger; (when I'm in need). But she ain't messin' with no broke da broke. Get down girl go head get down; (I gotta leave) Get down girl go head get down (I gotta leave) Get down girl go head get down;(I gotta leave). Get down girl gone head get down (I gotta leave). Get down girl go head get down (I gotta leave). Get down girl go head get down (I gotta leave). Get down girl go head get down (I gotta leave) Get down girl gone head get down!"

Steve's gaze fastened upon every sway of her hips. Steve's captivated by her, curvy waist and plugging neckline.

"Hey waiter, give the lady whatever, I mean, whatever she's drinking."

A few minutes passed and the waiter delivered the drink over to Julie. Julie turned in Steve's direction and grinned. She danced her way over to where Steve was sitting sipping on his beer. She slightly rubbed against Steve's chair.

He thought, "Wow, she's making it hard to relax looking at what she's working with. That dress is quite revealing and just downright sexy."

Steve's intoxicated eyes were fixed on every move of her alluring body. "Oh my God...look at that body."

"Hey handsome are you out by yourself tonight?"

"Yes I am, sexy! What's your name and, are you here alone?"

"I'm Julie, I'm out having some fun. Oh yeah, "thanks for the drink."

"My pleasure, sexy."

As they talk Julie remained standing while, occasionally swaying her hips to the sound of the music.

Steve attempted to place his arm around Julie's waist.

She pushed it away. "Whoa aren't we a little touchy feely tonight."

"I'm sorry but.... you are really looking hot."

"Thanks for the compliment but, take it easy."

Steve tried again to place his hand on Julie's waist and again she thrust it away,

"Oh are we playing hard to get or, oh no, don't tell me maybe men are not your cup of tea? That seems to be pretty popular these days."

"Funny, you can look but don't touch!"

Steve reached for Julie's wrist.

Julie slapped him! "Why do you keep putting your hands on me! I told you twice to stop it!" Julie throws her drink in his face.

"Woman, what is your problem?"

Julie shouts! "Buying me a drink doesn't mean you can put your hands on me. I didn't give you permission to touch me."

The bouncer came over to the table. "Is there a problem?"

"Yes!" She shouted. "This idiot keeps putting his hands on me."

"Sir, I think you've had enough to drink. Pick up your belonging and hit the road."

"Really, all I did was put my arm around her."

He pointed to the door. "Hit the road dude."

Steve shouts, "What! You can't throw me out of this bar I'm spending my money!"

"Hey dude don't make me put my hands on you. Get your stuff and hit the road!"

Steve snatched his beer. "Hey buddy, leave the drink."

"Man kiss my ass; I paid for this".

"Whatever! The back door is right there."

Steve stumbled to the door. Julie yelled, "Get out of here, you a-hole!"

"Yeah, Yeah, Yeah; good ridden, you crazy woman and kiss my ass too!" He waved his, bottle of beer in the air. Security shoved Steve out of the door.

Coincidentally, at the same time a young lady exited the grocery store across the street from the bar. Carrying a bag of groceries, making her way through a shared parking lot on her way to her apartment just up the street.

Steve stumbled through the sparsely lit parking lot. "Where is my car?" Steve noticed his vehicle sitting one row over. As he turned abruptly he bumped into the young lady.

"Excuse me, sir I'm sorry."

Steve stumbled and landed onto the hood of a parked car where he slid down landing on the ground. Steve's beer hit the ground breaking into pieces.

"What the hell!" The woman attempted to help Steve up.

In a drunken rage, He backhanded her in the face and knocked her to the ground unconscious. "Watch where you're walking, you stupid woman, you spilled my damn beer! That beer cost me my hard earned money."

The young woman lied unconscious between two of the vehicles. Intoxicated, Steve stood up with the assistance of the vehicles bumper next to him. He stood over her limp and lifeless body.

"That's what you get. You women think you run everything, I'll show you who's running things, you're going to pay me for my beer!" Steve unzipped his pants, drops down between the two cars, lifts the woman's skirt, pulls out his phallus and forces it into the unconscious woman.

"Now who's the damn boss? Now who's the man? I bet Kelly can't give you this, can she?" Steve grunted as he ejaculated. He grabbed a hold to the side of one of the vehicles as he lifts himself up off the woman. "Now that will teach you women not to F with me."

19

Steve zipped his pants and gathered himself, "Where's my beer." He stumbled to his car, got in and droves off leaving the woman lying on the ground unconscious with her skirt and panties disheveled and lying next to broken pieces of the beer bottle.

Approximately eight minutes later a woman passing by saw the victim sprawled on the ground. The woman pulled out her cell phone and dialed 911. Almost immediately the sounds of sirens could be heard approaching from a distance. Moments later the police and the paramedics arrived on the scene.

"Here she is over here!" They immediately began treating the injured woman helping her to regain conscious. The paramedics treated her facial wound then rushed her to the nearest emergency room.

The passer by told the officer, "I found her purse under the car along with her other shoe and a few of the groceries."

On the other side of town Steve pulled into the driveway of his house, tottered out of the vehicle, grabbed whatever he could to help his stability as he went up the stairs to the front door. He fumbled with his door keys, dropping them a few times on the ground. "Come on, Stevie boy, pull it together."

Steve walked into the living room, throwing his jacket on the sofa. The room was partially empty with only a sofa and a throw rug that barely covered the living room floor. He shook his head in disgust.

Up the stairs he pushed each door open as he passed them, looking to see his wife. But, Jennifer moved out just as she said.

"If that's how you want to do it good ridden, wifey, you'll come begging back once you realize how great you had it." Steve stumbled into his room, pulled off his shoes, barely unclothed before he was face down on the bed and fast asleep.

The alarm clock blared. A startled sleepy-eyed Steve doesn't smack the snooze button as he did earlier. The brightness of the morning sun pierced through the opening in the curtain. Wow, "I've got to get up and out of here!" Steve pushed the covers off of his leg, switched on the TV remote, and quickly headed for the shower.

Steve exited the shower wrapped in nothing other than a bath towel. While getting dress Steve hears bits and pieces of stories covered by the early-morning news report.

'In breaking news this morning a woman was found brutally raped outside of a local grocery store last night, the woman was discovered by a passerby who, heard the woman's muffled cries for help. The police are aggressively following up on some promising leads in the case. We will keep you updated as more information comes available."

Steve glanced at the television but hurried to finish dressing. As he hurried into an empty kitchen there was no sound of a blender, no coffee and no brown lunch bag waiting on the end of the counter.

"She'll be back."

He maneuvers around the side of the awkwardly parked car. "Wow, did I park like this? I guess I need to stop drinking!"

On the other side of town two plain-clothed detectives entered the hospital building where the victim Ms. Sandra Porter was recovering. The officers entered Sandra's room and found her sitting on the side of the bed robed in her hospital gown and gingerly sipping on a cup of tea. Sandra was still frightened and traumatized by the crime and extremely reluctant to speak to the officer.

"Hello Ms. Porter I'm officer's Sharon Demski of the New York Police department, myself and my partner; officer Darryl Nelson have been assigned to your case. I know you've been through a lot but; how are you feeling?"

"Okay I guess!"

"Ms. Porter we need to ask you a few questions about the events in the late hours of June fifteenth. I know this is difficult for you but by chance did you recognize the offender or, do you ever recall seeing him any time prior to last night?"

Visibly uncomfortable, "I didn't know him. From what little bit I do remember, I don't remember ever seeing him before that night".

"Can I call you Sandra?"

"Yes, that's fine."

"Sandra, I know this is hard for you but; is there any information you can give us about the perpetrator?"

"I didn't know him and, as much as I want to help you find this monster I am really not up for this right now."

"We understand how you feel. We will do everything we can to find the criminal who did this to you? We'll come back at a later time when you're feeling better."

Sandra laid back on the bed and bundled up in the fetal position pulling the covers up over her face.

"God why did this have to happen to me?"

CHAPTER 5

Jennifer had ignored Steve's phone calls. While Steve was at work Jennifer moved the remainder of her things out of the house and intentionally left her house keys on the kitchen counter.

A few mishaps on the job and missed deadlines had placed Steve's future with the company in jeopardy. His grooming habits had taken a turn for the worst. He rarely shaved and his clothes were often un-ironed and lightly stained with remnants of meals gone by. Steve had been hitting the bottle pretty hard attempting to drown away his sorrows and get past the pain of a failed marriage.

Sandra was still frightened about the whole sexual assault incident. The police continued to investigate interviewing witnesses, talking with the victim and; looking at video footage from other businesses in the area of the bar. The officers pulled the DNA from the rape kit administered to Sandra while she was in the emergency room and, they lifted a partial print from the broken beer bottle found at the scene of the crime.

Once the DNA tests are returned the officer believed that they had all of the evidence they needed to affect an arrest.

"I think we've got him!" After securing an arrest warrant from the Judge at the courthouse the officers headed to the suspects place of employment to make the arrest. The officers pulled up in front of the CDI Engineering Firm office building. On their way to the elevator they stopped by the security desk to request the assistance of building security.

"Good morning I am Officer Demski and I have an arrest warrant for one of the employees of CDI Firm a, Mr. Steve McDermott who works on the twelfth floor. We would like your assistance in effectuating the arrest of Mr. McDermott who is the primary suspect in a Sexual Assault and Aggravated Battery case."

"Alright officers; give us a moment please."

Turning to another building security officer on duty he says, "Tim can you assist us please? Hey Matthews; I need you to man this station until we return."

"Ok boss. Is everything alright?"

"Well, I don't know but we'll see once we get to the twelfth floor.

The four officers got on the elevator, press the button and quickly arrived at their destination.

"This way officers."

They exited the elevator and headed down the hall pass a row of offices where they came upon the receptionist Tammy; sitting at her desk

"Yes officers; is there something wrong?"

"Yes. We need to speak with Mr. Steve McDermott, is he in?"

Startled she responded, "Yes he's in let me let him know you're out here!"

Steve had just returned from lunch and, was sitting in his office looking over some documents.

"Steve, Tammy said, you have a visitor."

"Okay, who is it? Just send them in."

In walked two NYPD officers and two building-security officers.

"Are you Steve McDermott?"

"Who is asking?"

Alarmed by the guns and badges he said, "I am.

"Well, What's this all about?"

"Mr. McDermott, we have a warrant for your arrest."

"Me....are you sure?" The officers walked over to where Steve was standing.

"Steve McDermott, you're under arrest for the Criminal Sexual Assault and Aggravated Battery of Sandra Porter on the night of June fifteenth."

Taking out her handcuffs, officer Demski said; "Sir, I need you to turn around and place your hands behind your back."

"Hey, officer lady, this has got to be a big misunderstanding. Officers, you got the wrong person. I don't know what in the world you're talking about."

"Mr. McDermott, You have the right to remain silent. Anything you say can and will be used against you in a court of law. You have the right to an attorney. If you cannot afford an attorney, one will be provided for you without cost. Do you understand your rights?"

"Officer, I'm innocent, I didn't do anything."

"Well, that's for the Judge or jury to decide, you'll have your day in court. Step this way, sir."

Steve's boss and co-workers stood off to the side with arms folded, looking on with disgust. "Steve, this is it; your fired, you need to get you some help before it's too late."

"Mr. Scott, this is a terrible mistake Dammit. Officer, don't I get a phone call?"

"When the time is right you'll get one. Face the back of the elevator Mr. McDermott."

Steve is escorted out of the building and placed in the backseat of the squad. "Watch your head, McDermott."

"Hey, you got the wrong guy."

"Sir, you'll have plenty time to tell your story. For now I suggest you sit back and enjoy the ride."

"Well, that's impossible to do seeing that I'm riding in a squad car being charged with a crime I didn't commit. You guys are treating me like I'm a hardened criminal."

"When do I get to call my family? I do have a right to one phone call don't I?"

Officer Nelson from the front passenger seat said, "Do me a favor, McDermott, and close your mouth."

"Officers apparently you didn't hear me. I don't have any idea what you're talking about. As you can see, I'm a hard-working man with a great job. I haven't violated anybody's rights and, I gets it on the regular so I don't need to take it from anybody. I don't know what's going on but, you guys have arrested the wrong guy."

Back at the station in the lockup, "Have a seat, McDermott."

A table with two aluminum chairs is all that this room had to offer. The windows were elevated and shut tight. "Look, I'm not saying anything until I get a lawyer."

"Wait a minute Mr. McDermott, I thought we had the wrong guy, why you lawyer-ing up on me now? McDermott Listen, We can do this the easy way or we can do it the hard way. The choice is yours."

"Officers, the only thing I have to say is, I didn't do anything!"

Rising up from his chair he says, "Actually I've already called for a public defender and after you talk to them we'll have another conversation. Here's the phone: make your call. You got two minutes."

Steve frantically phones Jennifer "Come on Jennifer, answer the damn phone."

"Hello Steve, I need you to stop calling this number!"

"Who is this?"

"This is Kelly and I need you to stop calling Jennifer."

"Dammit, would you give Jennifer the phone please!"

"She told you before that she doesn't want to talk to you anymore."

"Hey, home wrecker, give her the phone it's an emergency and I need to talk to my wife. She is still my wife you know!"

"Well Steve I suggest that you find another wife because Jennifer is about to be mine. Jennifer doesn't belong to you anymore and you're no longer her problem."

"Dammit, put Jennifer on the phone!"

"Steve, I suggest that you move on with your life." "Don't make us get a restraining order to keep you away!"

"Look woman, man, or whatever the hell you are, I'm in jail and I need to talk to......."

Steve hears a loud beep. Steve slammed down the phone. Officer Nelson yelled, "Hey stupid, that's state supported property. Do you want another charge of criminal damage to state supported property?"

"Wow, I cannot believe this. This has got to be a nightmare!"

CHAPTER 6

After a few minutes of sitting in the interview room Steve was awakened. "McDermott, McDermott, get up, its time to speak to your mouthpiece."

"Hey officer lady can I get something to eat?"

"Its time to talk not time to eat. Mr. Public defender, he's all yours."

"Thank you, officer. Hello Steve, my name is Attorney Jeff Carr. I work for the office of the Public Defenders and I've been assigned to defend you against these charges. Here is a donut and some coffee."

"Mr. Carr, I didn't do anything."

"Well, Mr. McDermott, I've looked over the police report and I've been made aware of the list of key pieces of evidence and I must be honest with you, things don't look good for you right now. They have a video from an apartment building across the street that shows the perpetrator, who is a person who appears to look a lot like you. A parking lot camera produced a video of this same person. The video shows this person leaving the bar, stumbling into the parking lot, and bumping into the victim.

After being slapped by this person, it shows her falling to the ground, and the perpetrator stoops down between those same cars. Approximately three minutes later he gets up from the same spot the victim was found lying unconscious sometime later."

Raising his head Steve says; "Mr. Carr, that's all circumstantial evidence, we know videos can be altered? Sir, I went to the bar that night and, that's all I really remember!"

"Okay, there's also the people in the bar and the parking lot who, when interviewed and showed photos of you by the police, said you left out of the bar angry and upset a short time before the sexual assault took place. The profile and clothing description they gave matches, coincidentally, the man on the video, which I must say again, looks a hell of a lot like you."

"Yeah, well whose side are you on, that's all circumstantial evidence?"

"Well, they also have a lady named Julie from inside the bar who says, you sexually harassed her before you left the bar that night."

"Mr. Carr, I do remember leaving the bar because some broad was flirting with me but went crazy on me and had me thrown out when I tried to take her up on what she was offering."

"Mr. McDermott at the crime scene they also found a broken beer bottle lying next to the victim's feet, which the bartender verified that he sold you a beer of the same brand that night. However, they denied knowing how you left the bar with it. They were probably trying to protect themselves from any liability." Flipping through his notes he said, "Also, they sent the broken piece of the beer bottle off to the crime lab for DNA testing to see if it would match DNA that they will seek to take from you at some later point of time. Now, I'm on your side but the evidence against you is a tad bit overwhelming."

Steve grabbed the cup of coffee and slung it against the wall. "This is bullshit."

"I'm just telling you what they have against you."

Mr. Carr closed his files. In a few hours, we'll go before the Judge for what's called a bond hearing. The Judge will listen to the facts of the case, which the State prosecutor will present, your background if you have any and, the Judge will also listen to mitigation or, all of the positive things I have to say about you. He'll take all of that into consideration and then he will set a bond."

"Why?" Throwing up his hands up. "If they've got all of the evidence you're talking about then I must be guilty?"

"Steve the prosecutors will take anywhere from six months to a year to develop their case in their attempt to substantiate your guilt. At the same time, we'll work just as hard to prove your innocence. If you're able to pay the bond, you'll be free on bond during the pendency of this case. If you are not able to pay then, you will be held in custody during the duration of this case"

"Okay I was so drunk that night I don't remember much else. If they have all of this evidence then why wait a year for the inevitable? I want to plead guilty, pay for my crime, and be done with it."

"Well, Steve, you could get as high as twenty-five years in the penitentiary and a substantial fine."

A teary eyed Steve said, "Mr. Carr, I'm not a bad guy. Won't the Judge take that into consideration?"

"Listen, I'll tell you what, let's have the bond hearing today, then, if your decision is still not to fight these charges we will waive preliminary hearing, enter a plea of guilty, and set the case down for sentencing. This will give us a chance to get all of the evidence we can, finish our investigation, by then, all DNA test would have been completed, the police supplemental reports and witness statements will be made available to me and then we can make an informed decision if this is what you really want to do."

30

"Wow I was drunk and out of my mind, I don't remember most of what happened that night. But hey, if they have all of this evidence then I want to get this behind me and get back to my life."

"Steve, let's take our time with this and not rush through this?"

"Mr. Carr, I don't have that kind of time. Things have really been bad for me lately"

"Are you sure this is what you want to do?"

"Well, Mr. Carr, Sir, I don't want to prolong this any longer than it has to be." Placing his head in his hand. "I really need to get past this and move on with my life."

Mr. Carr stood. "I would advise against this but if you're sure that this is what you want to do, we'll have the bond hearing, I'll inform the State's prosecutor that we will be waiving all subsequent hearings and setting the matter for a plea of guilty and sentencing."

"Okay, let's get this over with!"

Attorney Carr grabbed his file and exited from the room leaving Steve sitting in his chair under the watchful eye of officers Nelson and Demski. "Wow. McDermott, I guess you do have a little sense after all."

Steve, laid on the bench and with tears in his eyes, eventually, fall off to sleep, Steve's sleep was overcome by reoccurring snapshots of the sexual assault. For the first time these snapshots take him back to the actual event. The dream displays the sexual assault.

"Watch where you're walking you stupid woman, you spilled my damn beer! That beer cost me some good money!"

The woman laid unconscious between two parked cars. "That's what you get! You women think you run everything. You're going to pay me for my beer. I'll show you whose running things!"

Steve unzips his pants and drops himself between the two cars, raises the woman's skirt, pulls out his phallus and forces it into the

31

unconscious woman. "Now who's the damn boss? Now who's the man?"

It was me! How could I do something so stupid? He couldn't believe that Jennifer did this to him! This was all her fault he reasoned!

CHAPTER 7

Since the arrest snap shots of Steve had been plastered all over the media that painted him as a monster who viciously attacked a helpless young woman in that quite neighborhood just after dusk on her way home from the grocery store.

Monster...Rapist....Women abusers, freak are just a few of the labels Steve's terrible actions had earned for him. As Sandra and her attorney exited their vehicle a local news reporter rush over to her.

"Mrs. Porter, how do you feel, what do you want to happen to the man who sexually assaulted you and left you for dead? How many years are you hoping for?" Sandra gave no response.

Today the judge will pronounce sentence on the monster that viciously violated this seemingly innocent, conspicuous woman. Today in the courtroom for the first time since the brutal rape Sandra Porter will come face to face with the monster who sexually assaulted her and left her body lying on the ground for dead."

Sitting behind Sandra is her mother and her long time friend; Melanie. Steve entered escorted by two sheriff's deputies. His hands were handcuffed in front and his ankles were in leg irons. Steve is adorned in an orange Erie County jump suit with **DOC** stamped on the back in bold black letters.

In a loud and boisterous voice the court deputy exclaimed, "Hear ye, hear ye, hear ye; this honorable branch of the circuit court of Erie County is now in session, pursuant to adjournment. The honorable Judge Darren Barker is presiding. There will be no talking while court is in session, you may be seated."

Sitting elevated in his oversized black leather chair, Judge Darren Barker sat centered between the proud symbols of the government, the U.S flag, and the Erie County flag.

"Good Morning, counsel we're here today in the case of the people of the State of New York verses Steve McDermott. To begin this sentencing hearing we will hear from the State prosecutors with their opening statement, Mr. Prosecutor you may proceed."

"Good morning your honor my name is Tom Duzek and I represent the people of the State of New York. This morning, we will hear of a horrible event, which has changed the life of a innocent, law-abiding woman who was minding her own business on her way home to have dinner with her boyfriend. The defendant, Steve McDermott a drunken, angry, vicious, carelessly selfish man exerted his demented will on this poor helpless victim. Your honor, not only did he assault her leaving her with an open gash to the interior portion of her lip and a bruised cheek bone but, he also brutally sexually assaulted her and left her lifeless body there on the ground bleeding and severely violated."

"Your honor while the State of New York does acknowledges the sober judgment of Steve McDermott in sparing this court and tax payers wasted time and, financial resources in a long drawn out trial. Justice still must be served and your honor for the sake of civil sanctity, punishment must be metered out in response to this terrible crime.

"At the end of this hearing we believe that we will have shown you that this man is not worthy of the freedoms that, civilized citizen in our society are, privileged to. As a result of his cold, careless, and calculated actions, Steve McDermott should be confined in a place designated for dangerous and demented criminals. At the end of this hearing, we will beg this court to sentence the defendant to the maximum sentence of twenty-five years in prison for the senseless crime of aggravated battery and criminal sexual assault, which he perpetrated on Ms. Sandra Porter."

"Thank you Mr. Duzek. Alright, Defense Attorney Carr."

"Your honor, if it please the court. Mr. McDermott sits here today accepting responsibility for the terrible mistake he made on the dreaded night under consideration. Not one time has he tried to avoid responsibility for his actions." Looking back at Steve he said, "your honor, Mr. McDermott was going through a lot at the time of this unfortunate event and he, quite frankly, lost control of his life. Mr. McDermott has absolutely no history of domestic abuse or any criminal activity. This unfortunate event was brought on by an alcoholic binge due to an untimely marital situation with his wife of three years whom he still loves very much to this day. Mr. McDermott has answered to these charges and is here asking the court to show leniency for this terrible mistake which, he is truly remorseful of.

"The defendant is twenty-four years old. He obtained a degree in engineering. He has worked for the last two years at CDI engineering firm. He volunteers each summer coaching little league baseball, which he has done for the past three years. At the age of twenty-four both of his parents died in a terrible automobile accident.

"Your honor we believe that a sentence which is fair, taking into account the seriousness of these charges while at the same time taking into account the mitigating factors surrounding this regretful event as well as the fact that Mr. McDermott has accepted responsibility for his wrongful deeds. We believe that the correct sentence should be a period of seven years in the penitentiary!"

The courtroom exploded with emotions.

Tom Duzek responded, "Oh my God he must be out of his mind."

The judge slammed his gavel and declared; "Quiet in this courtroom. The defense has the right to ask for what they believe is fair. Control your outburst or I'll be forced to clear this courtroom."

"Now...... Mr. Prosecutor will the victim be testifying during this sentencing hearing or, do you plan to put forth any additional aggravation?"

"Your honor the victim will not be putting forth anything. However, your honor, Ms. Porter although she insisted on being present for this hearing she has drafted a statement which she has asked me to read to the court."

Mr. Duzek stepped into the front of the courtroom. "Dear Judge, let me first thank you for the time and energy that you have given to this case which has devastated my life. On June fifteenth my life was turned upside down and unfortunately, I will never be the same. What this monster did to me has left me forever scarred and eternally damaged. I no longer feel safe in this world. I look around every corner. I wake up at night shaking. I triple check my doors and window locks. I feel stressed and sick often, I stay inside afraid to go out for anything other than work and; my family and friends constantly worry about my wellbeing. I was always taught to be a merciful person but what this monster did to me on that night has left me void of mercy. Your honor, please sentence this predator to a term in jail of nothing less than twenty-five years; so that he won't be able to bring this same kind of shame and torment upon anyone else. Thank you."

"Alright, Mr. McDermott, the law affords you the opportunity to address the court before I impose sentence. Would you like to say anything?"

"Yes sir." Steve stood up in front of his table, placed his note pad on the table closely in view. 'First, I would like to say, I'm sorry for all of the trouble I've cause Ms. Porter. I hope one day she will be able to forgive me for my terrible wrong. I would also like to apologize to the court for taking up its time and I guarantee this court that I will learn from this terrible mistake. I'm a much better person than my actions portray. I would greatly appreciate any mercy that this court can give me! Thank You Judge."

"Alright, I know that any amount of time I give as a sentence will seem excessive. However, I feel that time spent in prison should reflect the seriousness of the charges to which you are pleading guilty to and also serve to help deter others from such insensitive, cowardly and vicious behavior. Taking all of the evidence into consideration, the testimony, aggravation, and mitigation I must say, I am troubled by this tragic event and the carelessness shown to this innocent woman who by the way, did nothing to deserve this treatment. What kind of world do we live in where a person can't walk home from the grocery store without being accosted by someone with the intent of doing them serious harm?"

"I am however impressed that you have saved the court precious time and, the tax payer's money, pleading guilty to these charges and, placing this case in the hands of this court to render a Just and fair term of sentence. It is the opinion of the court that this is in fact an isolated incidence and, I do believe that Mr. McDermott has learned and will continue to learn from these horrific events. The court will sentence Mr. McDermott to, eleven years in the New York State Department of Correction. Upon your release from custody he will serve three years mandatory supervised release. Mr. McDermott, make good use of this time. Come out and do only good, to your fellow man."

Sandra Porter shook her head in disgust at the Judge's sentence.

Steve said, "Wow, this is the thanks I get for trying to be honest?"

"Finally, Mr. McDermott, you have a right to appeal this sentence within Thirty days of this hearing. If you cannot afford to prepare the appeal documents or hire an appeal attorney the court will appoint an attorney to prepare those documents for you free of charge. If the appeal is granted, the sentence will be vacated and any charges that were dismissed in consideration for this plea of guilty they will be reinstated and a new hearing date will be set. Do you understand your appeal rights, Mr. McDermott?"

Steve replied; "I do."

"Courts Adjourned. Good luck, Mr. McDermott."

Steve was handcuffed and escorted out and back to the lockup to await transport. In the audience was Steve's boss, Tammy, and his wife, Jennifer sitting with a blank stare on her face wiping her eyes with tissue.

CHAPTER 8

A few months had passed and Sandra was relaxing in the living room of her home. She had spent most of her days dressed in pajamas and sweat socks cuddled up with her television remote.

The doorbell rang "Who in the world is that? I'm really not expecting anyone nor do I want to be bothered with anyone." Eventually the rings turn into rapid knocks. The knocks kept coming. Finally, Sandra sneaked a peak out of the corner of the drapes and saw Melanie, her longtime friend standing there. Reluctantly she opened the door.

"Hi, Melanie."

"Hi, Sandra, it's been a while. It's like you just fell off the planet or something! I've been calling you but you didn't return any of my calls. I wanted to finally come by and see how you were."

"Oh, I'm well, I've just been trying to keep it together."

"Well, aren't you going to invite me in?"

"Sure, come in." As Melanie stepped through the door she noticed the living room table filled with dirty cups, empty potato chip bags and used paper plates. Sandra's hair was tied in a loosely knitted ponytail barely kept in place. "Have a seat, Mel"

As Sandra moved old newspapers and magazines from off of the sofa, Melanie asked, "Sandra, would you like for me to help straighten up things around here?"

"No, thanks, Mel, I plan to spend some time straightening up later today."

"Okay, would you like for me to go out and get something to eat?"

"No, I really don't have much of an appetite these days."

"Sandra, I know you've been through a lot but, you need to get out of this house and get some fresh air. I got a good idea, let's get you some clothes on and take a trip to the mall?"

"No, not today Mel I'm really not feeling that right now but; thanks for the invite. I've really been busy trying to finally get the paperwork into the bank for the bakery. I'm planning a grand opening early next year.

"How is that coming?"

"It's a lot of work but it's progressing along."

"How is mom?"

"She's okay, thank for asking Mel."

As Sandra answered the phone Melanie points indicating that she was going to use the bathroom. Melanie headed around the corner and down the hallway. Reaching for the toilet tissue she noticed an open wrapper of a pregnancy test kit in the trash can. Startled at the sight she picked the wrapper up.

"Oh my God, are you pregnant?" Holding the pregnancy test wrapper in her hand.

"Melanie, have you lost your mind or something?" Sandra pulled her sweatshirt down around her hips. "I've picked up a little weight but that doesn't mean I'm pregnant. A friend of mine and her husband are trying to have a baby and, she took the test while she was over here."

"Why would she take the test over here?"

"What, Melanie, are we an investigator or something, Miss Nosey? Maybe she wanted me there for support."

"Well, Sandra we've been friends for a long time and you know you can trust me, right?"

"I know, Melanie. You've got to excuse me, I've got to finish completing these papers." Sandra moved the conversation toward the front door.

"Okay, please call me if you need me for anything, I mean anything, okay?"

"Trust me, I will. Thanks for being a true friend Melanie." The two hug. Sandra closed the door and returned to her usual seat on the sofa. "God, you've got to help me through this."

CHAPTER 9

A few weeks have passed and Sandra was sitting in the doctor's office reading a magazine. Nurse Lacey said, "Sandra Porter."

"Yes."

"Please step into the examining room # Five and make yourself comfortable, the doctor will be in shortly. There is a restroom two doors down if you should need it.

"Thank you."

Finally, the doctor entered the room carrying Sandra's medical file. "Hello, I'm Dr. Montara, and I will be the doctor overseeing the birth of your child. I've look at all of your test results and everything looks fine. Based upon what I see I would estimate that you are between four and five months pregnant. Am I correct that you've filled out the form requesting to know the sex of your child?"

"Yes, doctor."

"Well, it's a boy!"

Sandra smiled. "That's really good news doctor."

"I've ordered more prenatal meds and please remember to take them faithfully. If there are no problems I'll see you in one month."

The 'Five months' brings her some relief from her hidden fear that her pregnancy is the result of the rape. She heads home with a new sense of excitement, believing that her baby is the son of her boyfriend Adam, whom she has not spent much time with of late.

"Hey, hey, hey. With the information maybe we can get back on track and be intimate again?"

After a few weeks Sandra phoned Melanie. "Hello Mel, this is Sandra." She was sobbing and, in a panic. "Can you come by here I really need you to take me to the hospital please?"

"Sure, what's going on?"

"I'm in too much pain to talk right now. I'll tell you everything when you get here, please hurry."

"I'm on my way right now."

Melanie rushed to Sandra's house. Sandra got in the car and the two headed for the hospital.

"What is going on, girl?"

"Mel, I'm in a lot of pain and I don't know why."

The doctor examined Sandra then told her what he had found. "Well, it seems the baby is very active. Nothing is wrong. The bleeding is slight and more than likely the result of some type of stress you're under. I need you to try and stay off your feet a little bit more. Maybe the child is practicing for the NFL or the NBA?" The two laughed. "Are you taking your meds?"

"Yes, I'm taking my meds doctor."

"A small dosage of Ibuprofen will be sufficient. Take care, and get some rest."

"Sandra, I knew something was going on with you! But, I'm your friend and you can count on my support through all of this."

"Thank you, Mel, that means a lot to me. I'm just worried that Adam won't be as supportive. I don't know if he's ready for a son yet especially, so unexpectedly like this."

"Oh Lord, it's a boy and you haven't told him yet?"

"No, he's been pretty busy with his job in and out of town so we haven't seen much of each other lately. I don't know if a son is on his agenda right now."

"Trust me, Sandra, no man can resist loving a beautiful baby boy."

"Yeah that's what I'm banking on."

A few days later, Sandra and Adam were sitting at a table in the restaurant where they placed their orders. Adam sat gazing across the room at the traffic coming in and, out of the door. "Waiter, can I have a glass of water please?"

Sandra said; "I'll have one too. Adam, I've really missed you."

"I know, my job has kept me busy but, I promise you, out of sight doesn't mean out of mind."

"That's good to know."

"Maybe, we can spend more time together now that things have slowed down for you. A lot has been going on and, I've got to do something about my Major League baseball addiction. I'm really excited about the Dodgers this season. I think this is the year we go to the World Series! That reminds me I've got to call about my season tickets. How are the plans for the second bakery coming?"

"Things are going well but unfortunately, I had to push my plans back to early next year due to some additional paperwork which the bank is requested."

"I know it's been rough on you but at least that court situation is behind you."

Sandra responded, "Yeah, I would really like for us to get closer and really take our relationship to a higher level."

"Hey, that sounds pretty good."

"Then honey, maybe we can have a bunch of children?"

"Also, what about a house with a picket fence and, don't forget about the station wagon! But seriously Sandra, all kidding aside I really would love to get a little further into my career before making any major family moves like that."

"Adam I have some great news."

"What's going on?

"My plans have really been put on hold because we're having a baby. I'm pregnant!"

Adam's mouth dropped. He lowered his glass with enough force to spill his drink. Dropping his head into the palms of his hands he said, "Sandra, please tell me, you're kidding?"

"No, honey, I'm five months pregnant and, we're having a boy."

"Oh wow you're serious! So this is what this quiet dinner is all about! Well, what are you going to do? Children are a huge responsibility and they need a lot of attention. I would say, we're both too busy for that right now! Wait a minute, how many months did you say you were? I don't really mean to be rude but, hell, are you sure this baby belongs to me? We haven't spent much time together over the last several months and, there was that unfortunate incident!"

"Adam, honey, you've been the only one in my life in a long while."

Adam sat back in his chair. "Wow, this is a lot to take in. Maybe I should go to the restroom. Here's the credit card and ID if the waiter comes back before I do with the bill."

Sandra's tears were no longer restrained. She picked up Adam's driver's license and looked on the back of it at the donor's sticker searching for Adam's blood type. She commits Adam's blood type to memory in order to make sure of its compatibility with the blood type of her soon to arrive, baby boy. When Adam came out of the restroom Sandra jumped up placing her napkin on the table. "Now it's my turn to go to the restroom." Sandra headed for the restroom.

Sandra arrived back to the table. Adam asked, "Are you finish with your meal? I've got a very busy day tomorrow so I better call it a night. Let me get you home!"

During the ride home Sandra pondered the idea of getting an abortion but she realized that she was too far along in her pregnancy.

In the driveway of her home, Sandra gets out of the car and walked to the door. "Good night, Adam."

"Okay Sandra, take care."

He backed out of the driveway. "Adam, call me!"

"This is too much stress for me. 'The thought of an abortion sounds really good to me right now. What am I thinking about?"

A few days later Sandra was sitting in her living room watching television. The phone rang. Sandra saw Adam's number. She smiled and grabbed the phone. "Hi honey, I miss you already!"

"Hey Sandra how's things?"

"Better now that I'm talking to you Adam! How about getting together tonight. We can finally have round two that we never got a chance to enjoy? Adam, I miss you so much."

"Hey, I wanted to call you with some great news I just got."

"I like good news. You sound excited, what's up?"

"I was offered a new job in Detroit. One of our warehouses is looking for a shift foreman and, my boss recommended me, for the position, which means, a raise in salary."

"Wow! Sounds like you've made your mind up."

"Sandra, I know this is a difficult time for you but I can't afford, to pass this up. "

Quietly sobbing she said, "Well, Adam what about the relationship we've been building over the last seven months?"

Adam responds, "We can still keep in touch. I know things are going to work out for you. You can always call me if you need me! Hey, I've got to let you go, I got a couple of deadlines I've got to meet. Let's keep in touch." Adam hung up the phone!

Sandra balled up on the couch. With tears in her eyes she shouted, "What in the world did I do to deserve this? I don't want to raise my son without his father. Dammit! He needs his father! I can't do this."

CHAPTER 10

Some months later it was early in the morning and Sandra was rushed into the birthing room at the hospital. Melanie stood next to her, wiping her during the timings of her contractions. Sandra was administered an epidural shot to help with the intensity of the pain but the relief came slowly.

"Wow, Mel, this little fellow is really trying to get out of there."

"Hold on, dear, we're almost there.

"Okay, Ms. Porter, I think you're ready. You're fully dilated and the contractions are coming at the correct intervals. Let's get that little guy out of there!"

Sandra closed her eyes and clinched her fist. "Okay, if you say so, doctor. I'm ready."

"Now, Sandra, when I tell you to, I want you to breathe deeply and push. Keep pushing until I tell you to stop. This is going to be a bit uncomfortable but I know you'll do just fine?"

Melanie said, "Don't forget your buddy is here and we can do this!"

"Okay, Sandra, at the count of three, I need you to push. One, two, three, now push!"

"Oh my God this hurts," Sandra screamed!

"Now push as hard as you can! Come on keep pushing. Breathe. Breathe! Push! Push!" Okay, the baby is almost here. I need you to stop pushing and, just take, deep breaths.

"Here we go, a handsome baby boy with all of his fingers and all of his toes." Sandra pants in exhaustion.

As the nurse gave the baby to Sandra, she said, "Oh my God, look at my, precious handsome little man."

"He's so handsome. What are you going to name the baby?"

"Jason. Jason Keith Porter. That's his name, Mel."

"That's a beautiful name and, Sandra, it fits him."

The nurse said, "Okay Sandra, Jason and I will go an get cleaned up and all checked out. We'll be back in a little while. You get some rest it's been a rough day for you." Lifting the baby's hands in a waving gesture, 'Bye Mommy.'

"Hurry back please!"

The doctor returned to the room. "Well, Sandra, how are you feeling?"

"I'm feeling fine doctor, thanks for all of your hard work."

"It was my pleasure." Looking over at Melanie he said, "And thank you for all of your help."

"Anything for my friend."

"Sandra, I'll go and get the results of all the preliminary test. No worries, I'm sure everything is perfect. He's a handsome healthy baby."

"Ok Doctor, how long before they bring him back?"

Moving toward the door "It won't be much longer. Let me go and get those reports and I shall return." The doctor left the room.

"Excuse me young lady. Do you have the reports for the, Porter Baby?"

"Just one moment doctor, I'm finishing it up now. I just need to record the blood type?" Ok, there it is. Oops!" The worker's cell phone rang again. "This phone is a hotline. Hello. Honey, what is it now? Honey, I'm really busy right now can I call you back in a few minutes? Okay sweetie, give mommy a few minutes."

She said, "Now, what was that blood type? I'm pretty sure it was, type AB. She logged it on the report as, type AB. "Here's the report doctor." Looking over at a co-worker she said, "This place, is really stressing me out. These doctor's, are always in a hurry."

Walking back into Sandra's room, "Okay Sandra, everything is good. You have a healthy, fully functioning baby boy. All of his vitals are perfectly, within normal range and his vision tests are normal. His weight is, eight pounds and ten ounces. You specifically requested to know the blood type of your child. His blood type is; type AB. Congratulations on a healthy child. Call the office and make and appointment for your month check up."

Sandra was shocked when she remembered Adam's blood type. "Oh God, Jason and Adam's blood types are not compatible." Sandra started crying.

"Is everything alright Sandra? Why are you crying?"

"Sorry doctor these are just tears of joy." Sandra wiped her eyes.

"Alright then, you make sure you, get some rest you've been through a lot. If everything maintains its normal course you will be released in the morning."

"Okay doctor."

Melanie asked, "Sandra what is wrong, you seem so down? I know you've been through a lot but you have a beautiful baby boy now."

"I know but, I've been having some doubts and, Dr. Montara just confirmed my worst fears. Fasten your seat belt Mel! Jason is not Adam's son!"

"OMG Sandra! I am so very sorry. Well, you don't worry about anything, I'll be with you and, the two of you will be, just fine. You have my word!

"Thank you. I appreciate that Mel. I know we'll be fine." She adds, "As far as I'm concerned, his father left me and my son all alone and that's the end of that! Hey, that's my story and dammit, I'm sticking to it!

"I'm going to leave and let you and Jason spend time alone, if you're okay?"

"Yes I am. You go and get some rest too. I will call you if we need anything!

"I love you Sandra and don't you forget that."

"I know you do Mel and we love you too!" Go and get some rest." Melanie left.

CHAPTER 11

3 Years Later

Bearded, Steve was sat in his prison cell sorting through papers. On the window ledge was a picture of him and, his ex-wife, whom he still retained hope of reconciliation. Steve picked up the picture, dusted it off, and placed it back. "Maybe when I get out of this hell-hole things can go back to normal?"

"Hey, Steve, you ready for chapel?"

"Yeah Ceelow, chapel sounds good. I need to get out of here for a while."

It was early Sunday morning and the decks of the prison were being mopped. However, not by Steve because he joined the religious group entitled, Changed Men, as a result this allowed him a pass on working or cleaning the decks. His evenings were spent in the library where he had renewed his love for reading. Steve tried to catch as much baseball and football as he possibly could during recreation time. Steve attended Sunday chapel, but sat unresponsive during the service; adding an occasional comment during discussions despite Pastor G's continued attempts to get him more involved.

"Good morning, class. No matter what we've become and where life finds us today, we're all the product of a created order. Whether you believe in evolution or a supreme being, which a large segment of our society refers to as God, we can all reach for that which we believe in and let it or Him help grow us into the valuable persons we were put on this earth to become."

"Yes Mike do you have a question?"

"I don't have a question but rather a comment. I don't know much about evolution or whatever but, I do believe we're all created by God, everything was created by God."

"Okay."

"You with your hand up, do you have a comment?"

"Yeah, hey you up front who just finished talking, he pointed to Mike, "what makes you so sure that this so called God, you talk about really, created everything?"

"Well, it's called faith but, you can't understand faith really unless you have it." It's a faith thing you wouldn't understand it!"

A few of the class members broke out into laughter.

"Alright we'll end this time together. See you guys next week. Be safe out there and, you guys, spend some time this week talking to your higher power and letting him talk back to you. You may be amazed at what He may say to you."

A few weeks had passed Steve was in chapel again, listening to Pastor G's discussion on the topic of forgiveness. "Forgiving yourself, forgiving others, and being forgiven by others is a process we all should engage in. We cannot go through life harboring resentment for others, or being over burdened with the resentment of others."

Steve reluctantly said, "Pastor G, I hear what you're saying but worrying about forgiveness is wasted energy."

"Well, I disagree, Steve. Un-forgiveness keeps us in a dark place and sometime distance from those whom we treasure the most."

"No disrespect, Rev, but that may work for you guys, but it's hard to even think about forgiving the person most responsible for me being here. Hell, I'm still struggling to forgive myself for being in this situation. Truthfully, I really can't care any less whether or not people forgive me or not. To hell with them!"

"Thanks for your honesty, Steve. However, in life we must make the decision to move past our mistakes and experiencing forgiveness from others is a real part of our human experience."

The discussion continued for the duration of the class time. "Alright we'll end this time together. You guys, spend some time forgiving others, and seeking forgiveness for yourself. See you guys next week. Be safe out there."

The next day Steve was lifting weights. Steve was not lifting by himself but others were using the weight benches, working out with the free weights, and working on their cardio. The aroma of serious workout and the clinking sounds of weight in motion filled the air.

Men dressed in white T Shirts displayed the successful results of their workout routines. There were well-sculpted bodies, triceps and biceps carved to penitentiary perfection. Rap music could be heard bouncing off the walls. Steve's buddy Ceelow walked over to Steve. Steve had buffed up quite a bit since arriving into the prison.

"Hey, man what, are you trying to lift the whole gym or something?"

"Come on, Ceelow, this is not a lot of weight! I'm just trying to look good when I get out of here and back to living in the real world."

Standing off to the side was his other friend Jay. "I know what you mean; Steve Schwarzenegger."

"Really Jay? If that was supposed to be funny you need some new material."

"Hey, Steve, did they tell you that the warden is looking for you?"

"No, man, they didn't. Jay, how long ago was that?"

"About an hour ago. He was up on the B deck asking around for you. He asked like he had something important to tell you."

Steve left in search of the Warden. "Hey, Steve, can you spot me?"

"No man I've got to locate the Warden; I'll be back;' in his Schwarzenegger voice.

"Oh now you've got jokes too." He laughed as he headed down the hallway.

"Maybe the warden had good news about my appeal. Steve walked down the corridors looking for Warden Blake.

One of the prisoner guards said, "He went that way about five minutes ago"

"Maybe they finally granted his appeal." He could feel it. "Something good is about to happen. Yes, Yes!"

Finally Steve located the warden in his office. Steve stuck his head into the door. "Warden, I was told you were looking for me. What's up?"

"Yes, I was, Steve. This came across my desk for you." He handed Steve a large yellow envelope.

"Thanks." Steve walked into the hallway ripping open the envelope. When Steve opened the envelope he saw that it was the finding of the appellate court. Located in the second paragraph, fifth line are the words: '**APPEAL DENIED!**' This court finds that your sentence is appropriate for the crime you were charged with and pled guilty to.

Steve returned to his cell, threw the papers across the room, and kicked the plastic trash container spreading all of the trash over the floor. Ceelow popped his head in the door. "Denied again, huh, Steve?"

"Yeah you know it! Hell with those arrogant, insensitive, neck tie wearing bastards."

"You've been here, what, about three years now? Keep your head up buddy. If at first you don't succeed try and try again!"

"No, that's it, man. This was my last hope. There is no higher court.

'Life is passing me by one day at a time all because of a stupid night of binge drinking and a home wrecker named Kelly. I'm not cut out for this life. I'm wasting my life away behind these walls. I need to get out of here and make things right. Funny, Pastor G's God didn't come through for me. Wow, looks like I'm here for the long haul."

"Man, those years will fly by before you know it! I've been here twelve years and, I've learned to take it one day at a time. We'll both get out of this hell-hole soon."

Steve responds, "I believe that, that's great Cee, just great. I don't want to die in here dealing with these fools and never get to what's out there waiting because of one bad mistake. These people act like I murdered somebody or something. There are people who killed other people and they got less than what I did.

CHAPTER 12

7 Years Later

It's been seven years since Steve was sentenced to prison, he's present for his parole hearing. Sandra was escorted into the hearing room through the administrative wing of the penitentiary. Her dear friend Melanie was sitting close by with Sandra's son Jason. Seated at the table with Sandra was a victim's witness advocate. Seated at another table was, Warden Blake, Steve's social worker, a member of the States Attorney's office, and a member of the New York State Parole Board. Steve was, escorted in by two guards. Steve was shackled at the ankles and placed in a chair at the table.

"Hello, everyone, I'm Mr. Waldron from the State parole board and, we're here today to conduct a hearing to determine whether or not Steve McDermott has met the qualifications for early supervised release. We have with us this morning; starting from the right: Mrs. Gutierrez... who is Mr. McDermott's prison social worker, Warden Blake, Warden of New York State Penal Institution, Tom Duzek from the State Attorney's office, and Mr. Richard Commons from the New York parole board.

Seated at an adjacent table was Mrs. Fitzpatrick from the victim witness office, Sandra Porter the victim, and across the room seated at the table is inmate Steve McDermott #05-4344568.

"We will hear from Warden Blake first. Warden Blake can you tell us what kind of inmate Steve McDermott has been?"

"Mr. Waldron, Sir, I haven't had any real problems out of inmate McDermott aside from his misuse of library time and his consistently keeping library books out too long. He's had a couple of light scraps with other inmates but all and all, he's been no real problem."

"Excuse me Warden."

"Yes, Mr. Duzek."

"Were there any weapons involved in these light scraps, as you put it?"

"No, there were not. However, during one of our surprise cell searches our officers did recover a handmade weapon, which when questioned about it inmate McDermott stated he keeps it for his own personal protection."

"Warden, these weapons are illegal, am I correct?"

"Indeed they are."

Across the room, Steve is shaking his head.

"Disciplinary actions were taken and Inmate McDermott paid for the violation."

"Okay, Ms. Gutierrez, how well has Inmate McDermott taken advantage of the rehabilitation programs offered to him?"

"Well, Mr. Waldron, he does attend chapel on Sundays. He has completed his 400 hours of anger-management courses and, he has completed only a couple of his counseling sessions with me."

"Ms. Gutierrez, in any of these sessions has Mr. McDermott voiced regret for his actions on the night in June fifteenth?"

"Not really. My own personal opinion if I may give it is Mr. McDermott would rather block that event out of his mind and not deal with it.

"Isn't that convenient." Mr. Duzek mumbled.

"Mr. Duzek, did you have something to say?"

"No, Mr. Waldron, however, I wish it was that simple for Ms. Porter who unfortunately has to spend the rest of her life dealing with what he did to her!"

"Okay does anyone have any more questions?" No one replies. "Ms. Porter, is there anything that you want to say or any questions you care to ask?"

"No Sir."

"Okay, inmate McDermott do, you want to make a statement on your own behalf?"

"Well, Sir, I would like to say that my time behind these walls has been a time of reflecting on why I'm here. I truly regret being here. While you all sit here judging me, I am not an animal, I'm a man who wants to be free and be a productive citizen in this society. I made a terrible mistake that I really regret. I ask you to let me get back to my life. I feel I've paid a severe debt for the crime I pled guilty to seven years ago."

"Alright, thank you, Inmate McDermott. I ask all participants to please submit your findings. I feel we have enough information to render a fair and impartial decision."

Shortly after this each panel member handed their voting slips to Mr. Waldron.

"Inmate McDermott will you please rise. It is the opinion of this board that significant rehabilitation has not taken place as of yet, and that you still lack a full appreciation for the crime you committed.

This board will re-convene in one year and at that time we will again take into consideration the level of your rehabilitation. This hearing is adjourned!"

Steve kicked his leg as he shouted, "What do you mean? That's ridiculous! This is a kangaroo court. I'll never be good enough for you insensitive bastards. Get me out of here." The officers placed Steve's hands behind his back, handcuffing him. "Dammit, this is wrong! I made a mistake don't you'll get it!"

As Steve was being escorted out, Sandra was being escorted out of the room as well. Down the hall Melanie and Sandra's son Jason sat waiting. Steve noticed Sandra in the hallway hugging a young child. Steve was shocked! "Where did he come from?"

Steve's anger at the board's decision was quickly replaced with a smile. Steve thought, that could possibly be his son. Steve becomes convinced that the boy is the illegitimate son of the rape he committed seven years ago.

Early the next morning, Steve headed for the library. The librarian said, "Good morning, Steve, you're early this morning."

"Yeah, I am, I couldn't sleep thinking about some information I need. Are the computers logged on yet?"

"Yes they are. Don't forget about the two hour time limit."

"Yeah, I remember!"

Steve walked down the aisle passing several bookshelves before he took a seat in the computer booths located in the back left corner.

"Okay now, let's see what's going on with Ms. Sandra Porter. Good, there isn't a lot of Sandra Porter's living in Uptown New York. Wow, it's amazing the amount of information you can get on the world-wide web these days." He navigated through various pages and websites. "Sandy does San Diego...where did that come from?"

"Okay, here's a picture of a October 2007 Grand Opening of Bright Start Bakery proprietor, Sandra Porter. Hum, nice place and nice pictures. "Sandra Porter of Uptown New York opens a new morning spot where commuters and those early morning risers can have easy access to a cold or hot breakfast snack. "Bright Start Bakery specializes in many of your most-loved baked pastries. The bakery also has intimate breakfast nooks with daily newspapers and HD televisions screens available for those with time to spare. Stop in and start your day off 'Bright.'

The caption under the picture read: "Sandra and her close friend, Melanie;" "Sandra and Loan Officer Ms. Emile Walton of Fidelity Bank," "Sandra, her mother and Jason her two year-old son. "

Hey, not a bad-looking kid."

The librarian approached. "Excuse me, Steve, you have about five more minutes left on the computer."

"Okay, I'm shutting things down in a minute."

"Thank you Steve."

"Sandra's actually not a bad looking girl? I think I'll just print this picture and hang it up in my cell. Wow! My son! I would have preferred Steve Jr. but Jason will have to do."

In his cell, Steve cuts Sandra out of the picture and taped the picture over his bed.

The next morning Steve was back at the library gathering all the information he could on fatherhood and good parenting. Steve bargained with the other inmates for their library time so that he could continue his research.

The Chesapeake county public records provided him with the birthdate and vital statistic of Jason, including his exact birth date, blood type and birth certificate. The birthdate matches the approximate time scheme of his sexual assault.

"According to this information we're a perfect match."

Tears filled Steve's eyes. That night, Steve fell off to sleep starring at the photo of Jason and contemplating on the many things he hoped to be able to do with his son once he was released from prison.

Sandra get ready for a fight for rights to my son!"

CHAPTER 13

A few days later, Steve leaned in the door of Mrs. Gutierrez's, the prison social worker's office.

"Good Morning, Mrs. Gutierrez, can I come in?"

"Yes, come in. I haven't talked to you since the hearing, how are you?"

"I'm doing okay."

"I've got a kind of off the-wall question for you. Do they offer any parenting classes in here?"

"Yes we do. Parenting classes meet the first and third Tuesday morning at nine o'clock, and if memory serves me correctly, you don't have any children so, you're planning ahead for the future?"

"Well, Mrs. Gutierrez you just never know."

"Steve, children are a major responsibility and they don't come with manuals so any help you can get while you're here will be worth it."

"You're right, that's why I'm here talking to you."

"Should I sign you up to start next Tuesday?"

"I'll be there with bells on!"

ONE WEEK LATER

"Good morning class, I'm Dr. Stanley Davis, affectionately called Dr. D. All of you here have expressed an interest in being better parents while your incarcerated and after you leave."

"These classes will better equip you to be good parents and to understand the awesome responsibility of raising children. I have three children and all of them require something different and differing levels of attention. Understanding how the mind of a child works is key to good parenting. At the conclusion of this course you will better appreciate your role as a parent, and appreciate the necessity of two parents actively involved in the life of a child. Now, does anyone have any questions or comments so far? Inmate Brown."

"Yes Sir Dr. D. How do you get children to appreciate their father even if they have a bad past?"

"Well, you have to earn that respect by changing your ways and showing them that the old you no longer exist."

"Dr. D."

"Yes, inmate Meyers."

"If I'm correct, it's hard to shield children from all that the streets and the hood has to offer? How do I keep them from going down the same road I did?

"You must be willing to spend time with your child in order to lead them down the right path. If you don't lead them, all of you are living proof that someone or something else will."

"Yeah Dr. D, I know that's right!"

"Yes, Inmate McDermott. You have a question?"

Steve asked, "How important is it for the father to be involved in his kid's life?"

"Good question. Both Parents are equally as important. Both the mother and the father bring various skills and benefits to the parenting experience. Since biologically, children are the exact blue print of their parents, when parents are involved they can easily identify areas of flaw, because one of them has exhibited the same type or similar behavior in the past. Having the benefit of both parents provides for a balanced attack at fighting wrong behavior and fortifying right behavior. Often in the parental experience, one parent tends to compliment the other so that the child's development is thorough and complete. Great question, Steve."

"I'm Mike and, when I hit the bricks this time I want to do better by my kids. I don't want my son and daughter to go through what I went through."

"That's good, Mike. Children imitate what they see others do especially their parents."

Dr. Davis looked at his watch and stated, "Good conversation today. We will meet again in two weeks. Please read over the handouts and write down any questions that you may have."

Steve returned to his cell and was visited by his friend Jay. "What's up, man? What's this I hear about parenting classes? The word is, you're acting like you just hit the lotto or received a pardon from the President? You never mentioned anything to me about a child. Don't you think you might be putting the cart before the horse?"

"Listen man, you're one of my closes friends in this Hell-hole. What I'm about to tell you stays between you, me and, these brick walls, deal?'

"This sounds serious, deal. I'm all ears!"

"Listen, man at my parole hearing my victim had her seven year-old son with her. I've been doing some research and I'm thoroughly convinced that her son is actually my son."

"Wait a minute. Wow, what makes you so sure the boy is actually yours?"

"In all of the pictures I found of her there is no mention of a husband, boyfriend, or father. Look at this picture. What do you think?"

"Well, he sure does have your big head." The two shared a laugh.

"Oh now you got jokes! The boy's age matches up with the time of the crime. I also accessed the Erie County records of vital statistics and found out his blood type is compatible with mine. All of that, plus my gut feeling, tells me he's my son!"

He pointed to the picture. "Seriously, Steve, truthfully speaking, he could pass for your son, but what good is that? Hey, that look in your eyes tells me you're up to something, you've got a plan don't you?"

"Yeah, I plan to be my son's father, that's all, nothing else. When I get out of here I plan to, claim my son and be a real part of his life. Pastor G. always says, "God works in mysterious way."

"Man, you've stooped to a new low, using the Reverend's words to support your plan." The two shared another laugh as Steve swore his buddy to secrecy.

"Man, truthfully I doubt that your victim would ever let this happen."

"Well, it's really not about her, it's all about being in the life of my son! Doesn't that have a nice ring to it? "My son."

"You sound like you really mean it, Steve?"

"Yeah, I think it's time, that I do the right thing and try to make up for, my mistakes!"

"Man, I'm touched, now let's go touch some weights in the workout room."

Another Sunday morning rolled around and Steve was attending chapel services. The topic of discussion was; making mistakes, but Steve managed somehow to move the discussion back in the direction of forgiveness. "Pastor G, I've got a question." Steve asked, "Once you've forgiven yourself, how do you get others to forgive you?"

"Well, you've got to earn the respect you've lost through your actions. If your actions got you in to trouble, use your actions to get you out of trouble. Most people who we've wronged are not concerned about our words, it's our actions they really care about."

"Is it as easy as that Pastor G?"

"Well, no, it can be a daunting task but make the decision to change, stay focused on your goals, and make a strong commitment for your success. There is a strong likelihood that those who have been victimized by our action will be more understanding and forgiving when they see our determination to get things right. Mahatma Gandhi said, "The weak can never forgive. Forgiveness is the attribute of the strong."

"Thanks Pastor G. I don't know a whole about Gandhi but, you're not half-bad after-all.

Pastor G. stated, "All right, guys make the best of this week. I'll see you next Sunday."

Steve returned to his cell and, against the advice of Jay, wrote a letter to Sandra, using the address of Sandra's New York bakery. Steve begged for Sandra's forgiveness, explaining the situations surrounding the night of the crime. Steve mentioned the devastation of his wife leaving him for another woman, the demands of his job and the alcohol abuses that severely influenced his actions on the night of the crime. Steve admitted that these precipitating circumstances are not excuses for his criminal behavior but only contributing factors.

Steve closed the letter clearly confessing his desire to be a father to her son and told Sandra of his belief that Jason is his son, and if given the chance he believes he could prove that he is a changed man and that, he could be a good father to Jason.

CHAPTER 14

At her bakery, Sandra was conducting inventory for the morning of the pastries and donuts in the display cases. The door opened and in walked the mailman with a stack of letters that he handed to her. "Hello, Sandra here you go." Sandra flipped through the letters and came upon one addressed to her from the state penitentiary, baring the sender's name of, inmate Steve McDermott.

"What the hell is this?"

Sandra quickly threw the letter into the trash can but decided reluctantly to keep and show it to the police, who, she hoped, would stop any further communication from Steve McDermott. However, when she contacted the police they informed Sandra that based upon her not opening and reading the letter they have no reason to believe that the letter contained anything of a harassing or threatening nature, therefore there is no crime committed. She stated that she didn't want to give her rapist the satisfaction of hearing anything that he had to say.

With tears in her eyes Sandra phoned Melanie. "Hello, Mel, can you believe that asshole, rapist sent a letter to my bakery? What makes him think that I want anything to do with him?"

"OMG, San, how dare he? Did you read it, and what did he say?"

"Hell no! I am so mad. I'm not interested in anything that he has to say?"

"Girl, are you going to be alright? Do you need me to come to the bakery?"

"No I'll be fine. I'm just pissed off at this pompous idiot! It's almost time for me to leave to pick up Jason anyway."

"How are things going at the bakery?"

"Things are well. However, Jason is a different story. Trying to run a business and raise a son is an extremely tall order."

"How's school coming for him?"

"He's doing fine as long as I stay on him. He really wants to play sports. All he talks about is baseball and playing on the neighborhood little league team but; I just don't have the time."

"Well, San, what's going on with you and who's playing on your team hint...hint...hint?"

"Nothing and nobody!"

"Girl, you need to find you a good man who can help you with Jason and help you release all that built-up pressure."

"What pressure are you talking about, Mel?"

"You know, that personal pressure below the naval. Hint, hint?"

"Girl, Jason and this bakery is my main concern, and besides that they've invented other ways for a girl to release that personal pressure, and thankfully Wal-Mart's got a sell on batteries hint, hint, hint.

"Girl, I know exactly what you mean."

"Thanks for making me laugh, Mel."

"That's what friends are for."

"Can you believe that? The nerve of that crazy fool to write me! I got to finish up and get out of here. I'll talk to you later."

Once Sandra got home she placed the letter in a storage bin which she kept in the bottom of her closet. "He doesn't have a clue who the hell he's messing with!"

CHAPTER 15

Another year had passed and Sandra was being escorted into the hearing room adjacent to the penitentiary. Her friend Melanie was there for support but waited outside in the hall.

"Hello, I'm Mr. Waldron from the State Parole Board. We're here today to hold a hearing to determine whether or not Inmate Steve McDermott has met the qualifications for early release. We have in attendance all of the necessary participants for this hearing and of course; inmate Steve McDermott #05-4344568.

"First, we will hear from Warden Blake. Warden Blake, can you tell us what kind of inmate Steve McDermott has been in the last twelve months?"

"Mr. Waldron, I haven't had any problems out of Inmate McDermott. Fortunately, he has really busied himself with personal-enhancement classes improving himself and showing sure signs of change. From all available evidence, Mr. McDermott seems to have turned over a new lease on life and made significant strides in his rehabilitation. He's been a great help in the library and he still spends most of his time reading books and meeting with self-help counselors."

"Thank you, Warden. Okay, Ms. Gutierrez, how well has Inmate McDermott taken advantage of the various programs we have to offer?"

"Yes, Sir. Well, I have to agree with Warden Blake he has been a model inmate for the last twelve months. I must admit I've been impressed with his change in attitude. That's all I have, Mr. Waldron."

"Okay, does anyone else care to add anything to this discussion? What about you Mr. States Attorney?"

"No, unfortunately I don't have anything else to offer."

"Alright, with us again today is Ms. Porter. Ms. Porter is an important part of what will take place here today. Ms. Porter, is there anything that you want to say or any questions you would care to ask of this board?" She shook her head looking away from Steve.

"Very well."

"Inmate McDermott, do you want to make a statement on your own behalf?

"Yes, sir. Thank you for this opportunity to speak. My time behind these walls has been a time of reflecting on how and why I ended up in here, and I truly regret doing what I did to get here, I know it was wrong and I pray for forgiveness from this board and from Ms. Porter. I'm looking forward to one day getting back to being a productive citizen in this society which I know I am capable of being. There are some important things and people waiting on me out there and I'm a better man now. If this board should see fit to grant me an early release, I promise that I will never return to this place. Thank you all.

"Thank you, Mr. McDermott."

After a few minutes Mr. Waldron stated; "Well, I think we have enough to make our decision. Inmate McDermott, it is of our opinion that rehabilitation has taken place and having said that, this board is

73

in agreement with granting you early-release. After your documents are completed and early release processing is finished, you will be set to be released. Be careful as you migrate back into society. You will have to walk a fine line. Don't mess up this privilege. Of course there will be guidelines that you must follow. Any violation of these guidelines will cause you to be back in custody. You appear to have really turned things around so, keep up the good work. Make it your business to avoid whatever it was that caused you to end up in here. Congratulations, Inmate McDermott! Meeting adjourned."

With tears in his eyes Steve could hardly speak. "Thank you all for giving me my life back and giving me a new start."

After eight years, Steve was finally released on parole and placed back into society with restrictions.

"McDermott, believe me, as your Parole officer we will not hesitate to haul your behind back in the joint, and if you don't believe me, just try me. Walk softly or you will fall hard. Stay out of trouble. Keep your nose clean. We'll be in touch, McDermott, I promise we will!"

A week later Steve was successful at finding an apartment. He moved into a one-bedroom apartment. The next day Steve contacted his old employer trying to find a job. "Hello, Steve it's great that you're out and back into society. How may I help you?"

"Mr. Scott, I need a job and I would appreciate any help you can give me"

"I'm sorry but we don't have any openings in this office but call this number, ask for Mr. Bentford and tell him I gave you his number. They might be able to do something for you. Other than that, how are things going for you?"

"Thanks for asking, things are going well so far, I've just got to take it one day at a time."

"That sounds like a good plan."

"Yeah, but I need a job so that I can get back on my feet."

"Well, give me a call and let me know how things go."

"Ok Mr. Scott, I'll keep in touch and thanks for the help."

Steve lands a job with a start-up marketing firm. One month later, Steve was seated in his new office. Steve placed a phone call to Sandra at her bakery. "Hello, may I speak to the owner, Ms. Sandra Porter."

"Okay, may I tell her who's calling?"

"The building code Inspector."

"Alright, Sir, hold on one moment. "Sandra there is some guy on the phone who says he's a building code Inspector."

"Hello, this is Sandra Porter, how may I help you?"

"Hello Ms. Porter please don't hang up the phone. This is Steve McDermott and I need to speak with you briefly."

"How the hell did you get this number and, how dare you call this phone? I have absolutely nothing to say to you. Please stay out of my life and dammit, don't call here anymore!"

"I know Jason is my son and I really want to be an active part of his life."

"Are you crazy? Jason is not your son and, if he was you still wouldn't be allowed anywhere near him, you pompous bastard! Evidently all that time in prison has destroyed what little brain you did have."

"Listen, Ms. Porter, I don't mean you any harm I just want to be here for my son. "

"Listen you crazy, psycho rapist, if you call me or write me again, or if you come anywhere close to me and my son, I will have you arrested and shipped back to that hell hole you called home for the last eight years. Do you understand me? I won't hesitate to notify your parole officer that you're harassing me and my family!"

"Sandra, please don't do this, I've did my time. I know what I'm talking about. I just want to be an active part of my son's life, that's all!"

"Stupid he's not your son and have you forgot what you did to me?"

"Sandra, I'm truly sorry for the mistakes I made but, I know he's my son!"

"How dare you call me, you monster, with this insanity? Haven't you done enough to ruin up my life?"

Sandra slammed the phone down. Later that afternoon Sandra reached out to Steve's parole office.

"Hello my name is Sandra Porter and I'm the victim of one of your parolees, Steve Mc. Dermott and he's been, calling and harassing me. I know that's a violation of his parole and I need you to, haul his no good behind, back into prison."

"Well miss, has he threatened you in anyway?"

"No he hasn't."

"Well, as long as, he's not committing any crimes our hands are tied. McDermott's requirements are, to checks in once a month and, report that he has found and is maintaining employment and most importantly, staying out of trouble. So far, he's been no problem."

"Dammit, making phone calls to the victim is, a problem! Well, please call him and tell him I don't want to have anything to do with that rapist creep." This has got to be a violation of something?

"That's not a violation. If that changes we'll be happy to haul his behind in and send him back to prison on a violation. My name is Officer Wallace and feel free to ask for me when you call."

"Yeah, thanks for nothing. You've been no help to me at all."

"Have a nice day Ms. Porter!"

Later that morning Steve was thumbing through the phone book, he ultimately placed his finger on an ad for a father's right attorneys and made an appointment.

Steve arrived at the Attorney's office dressed in a suit. "I'm here to see Attorney Larry Daniels."

"Okay sir what is your name?"

"Steve McDermott."

"Have a seat and he'll be right with you."

Mr. Daniels emerged from the back "How are you Steve? Let's go into my office." The two head for his office.

"Let me warn you Mr. Daniels this is certainly not the usual set of circumstances."

"Believe me Steve, I've just about heard them all!"

"Okay, here we go." Steve told him about the rape, his son, and his desire to claim parental rights for the son.

"Wow, Steve. Fortunately for you, these are just the kind of cases we like to handle. Let me ask this, how does the mother feel about this?"

"Well, that's the problem. She's totally against it and won't have anything to do with me. She won't respond to my letters, she hangs up when I call, and the thought of me being in Jason's life makes her blood boil!"

"Again, that's probably to be expected Steve but; despite your tangled web, you're still the child's father and that does count for something. The desk clerk will give you some forms to fill out. I will take your case and file the necessary motions. The charge to represent you will be $5.000, half due when we file, and the other half due once we win. I think you have a good case and despite the action that precipitated this case; I believe people will jump on your side and we will win. For some reason people today are sympathetic to these types situations."

"That's awesome, Mr. Daniel and I promise I'll work on paying you the fees."

"Hey, look into social media as a means of raising awareness of your case and maybe even raise the eyebrows of donors who have the means to help you obtain your rights as a father.

The next morning Steve started a fan page on Facebook and opened a twitter account where he outlined his story and solicited for financial supporters. Over the next few weeks, some social media responses were pleasant and some were vulgar and downright nasty. "Get a life, you insensitive bastard" "What are you trying to do, raise the boy to be a rapist like you? In box me so I can show you how it feels to have something shoved up in you."

"Okay, now this is more like it."

A few responses read, "The boy does needs his father if that's your goal then I wish you the best." "I think it's a good cause, I'm in, here's my donation." "Hey, you sound like a really great guy. Let's meet so I can give you some more sons to raise that you won't have to fight for. Call me ASAP." To Steve's surprise, an anonymous person donates $1.000 dollars toward his defense fees, posting, "Every boy needs his father in his life. No kid should have to go through what I went through, not being allowed to get to know or spend time with my dad."

Each day brought more funds and also more negative comments. When the amount nears $10.000 and word started to spread on social media about the nature of the case, the media soared. Steve started to get phone calls from newspaper outlets, talk shows, and many others wanting to highlight Steve's custody battle. But he wasn't trying to be famous;

"I'm not in it for a book deal, I'm just trying to be a father."

Meanwhile when Sandra received notice of the filing of the case and the date for hearing she was irate. "How dare this idiot disrupt my life? What is this psycho trying to accomplish with this foolishness? My son and I will be just fine without any help from him. This will happen over my dead body!"

CHAPTER 16

Outside the County court building the local media was on hand. Father's right groups were lined up in support of Steve and many of the supporters were wearing matching T. Shirts. A few of them were holding up signs that read: "A Good Father Equals A Good Son." "Protect the Boy's Rights Give Him His Father." Mother's right support groups and women support groups lifted their signs: "Mother's Have Rights Too" And, "The Boy needs a Mother not A Monster."

Ms. Chase, Sandra's Attorney was well known for her snazzy dress, and true to form she was wearing a two-piece blue pinstripe pants suit and three inch pumps. Her blood hair moved about with every shift in her argument.

Steve's attorney Mr. Daniels met Steve in the front of the court building. A reporter moved over to Steve to get a statement. "Mr. McDermott, my viewers want to know what do you hope to accomplish here today?"

Steve responded, "My only desire today is to be a father to my son. Statistics show that young boys need their father. They also show that boys raised without their fathers in their lives have a greater chance of being involved in negative behavior leading to the commission of crimes. I don't want my son to go down the same road, unfortunately, that I did. I've been punished for my crime and did my time, and I don't think it's fair to punish me for trying to be a father. Two wrongs definitely don't make a right!"

"Mr. McDermott, what about the fact that the boy you refer to as your son is the product of a brutal rape where the boy's mother was left by you for dead? And I have to ask this, how are you so sure the boy is actually yours?"

"Well, I've paid for my crime. I made a mistake in what I did, and I accept full responsibility for my bad actions. And to your second question, I did my homework and researched my son's medical records along with my attorney as well and the proof of paternity is unquestioned. That's the only reason why we stand here today!"

"Okay, last question. If the judge does see fit to grant you visitation of your son, do you think you'll ever be accepted by the boy, or be able to get along with the boy's mother?

"Right now it's not about her, it's about my son!" Into the courtroom they walked.

"Good morning everyone, I must admit after reading your motion, Mr. Daniels you certainly have shown tremendous boldness in filing this case, maybe even to your client's detriment."

Mr. Daniel's said, "That's true, your honor, but what we have here is a man who has only one request of this court, one single desire in life, and that is to be involved in the life of his son."

"Excuse me your honor, we vehemently object to this unnecessary line of discussion! My client, Ms. Porter, has gone through enough already, and we believe that this request is being presented as a means of perpetuating Ms. Porter's pain. This man committed a calculated, brutal sexual assault and now he wants to burden this court with this ridiculous pursuit for selfish gain."

"Judge Dowden, can you please tell Ms. Chase to let me finish talking before she so rudely cuts me off?"

"Alright, you two enough of the cat and mouse games. What I need to hear is specifics as to whether or not Mr. McDermott's involvement in the boy's life will have a negative or positive effect. I've read each side's response to the motion so I am fully aware of your positions. Let's hear from your witnesses please."

Sandra's friend Melanie was called to the witness stand.

"Hello, Your Honor, my name is Melanie White. Your Honor, the last eight years have been rough for Sandra. She has endured some major struggles but she managed through some hard work and a lot of help from the Lord to get back up on her feet. Sandra is a great mother and in no need of help from this man."

"Your Honor"

"Yes Mr. Daniels."

"We would like for the court to be aware of the fact that Ms. Porter is a business owner and running her establishment takes a lot of time and effort. This is one of the areas where we believe our client will serve his son well. This is not about Ms. Porter and my client but rather, about my client and his son.

"Wow, this is so interesting, Mr. Daniels, but, Your Honor, we also cannot forget that this man brutally raped Ms. Porter eight years ago. He left Ms. Porter lying in a parking lot to die. This is not and I stress not, the kind of man who needs to be in the life of this child. The petitioner didn't even turn himself in for this crime. This man caused problems while he was in prison, he has a history of alcohol abuse, and he violated at least the spirit of his parole by being in contact with Ms. Porter. Judge this family has been through enough."

"Your Honor, please don't place anymore undue stress on this woman and her child whom, by the way, she adequately cares for by herself, and contrary to what Attorney Daniel feels, she is doing a good job."

The judge responded, "Well, it's good you bring that up. Let me ask you Ms. Chase, how well is the boy doing in school? What does his grades look like?"

"Your Honor, he's doing very well. He's a B-average student. My client is only asking for her and her son to be allowed to live their life without any intrusion by Steve Mc. Dermott. Thank you, judge."

"Ms. Chase, would your client like to make a statement?"

"Yes, Your Honor Ms. Porter would like to have something to say."

Sandra rose from her seat. "Your Honor, I would like to say that, I have been through a lot in the last eight years and it has not been easy dealing with the crime that was committed against me. However, I've done everything possible to pull my life back together and raise my son. I don't feel I need anyone to help me raise my son. This man has done enough to make my life miserable. Because of the shame of who his father is, I chose to tell my son his father left us when he was very young and my son has accepted this as true. Please don't send him or me through another rollercoaster of emotions by allowing this criminal into our lives. I'm afraid of him and I fear my son will be also. I've managed to raise my son even though there were times when we didn't really know where our next meal was going to come from. Thank you, judge."

"Mr. Daniels, would you care to add to this discussion?"

"Yes Your Honor." He placed his left hand on Steve's shoulder. "Mr. McDermott has had a rough life as well. Infidelity, the death of his parents, divorce, alcoholism, pressures on the job, eight years in prison, and now a battle for the one thing he has left in this world, Jason, his son. Your Honor, most of the aggravation is true but Mr. McDermott has paid for that terrible mistake."

"The Prison board found that he was rehabilitated and released him early on probation. One of the board members even referred to Mr. McDermott as a model prisoner. Mr. McDermott is willing to abide by any conditions which this court deems necessary. The court is fully aware of the need for the father to be in the life of the child, be it a boy or a girl. However, these needs are increased when the offspring is a male child."

"Steve, Mr. McDermott is simply a good guy who made a bad mistake. Prior to his incarceration, before this isolated incident, Steve was a model citizen. Mr. McDermott holds a degree in engineering and has maintained steady employment. He has also successfully completed extensive alcohol rehab treatment and has been sober for the last eight-plus years. He completed eighty hours of anger management, and two hundred hours of parenting classes. Mr. McDermott is a reformed man. As a society we should be proud because in the case of Mr. Mc. Dermott, the system worked. He's reformed, and he's rehabilitated.

"Your Honor, Mr. McDermott has made a one hundred and eighty degree turn since the unfortunate events of June 15, 2005. Your Honor, we're calling on this court to do what's right, what's fair, and what is best. Let this man be a part of his only son's life. Thank you, Your Honor." Mr. Daniels took his seat.

"Alright, Mr. McDermott, would you care to add anything to this discussion?"

"Yes, Your Honor. First, I apologize for any inconvenience I've caused you and this court today. Judge, my only desire today is to be a father to my son. Boys need their father. Statistics show that boys raised without the fathers in their lives have a greater propensity toward criminal activity. I don't want Jason to go down some wayward path as I did."

"I've been punished for my mistake, and I did my time. I'm sorry for my misdeeds and wish I could undo what I did but I can't. I don't think that it would be fair or right to penalize me for trying to be a father to my son!" Tears filled his eyes. "Judge, just let me make up for my past mistakes and prove that I'm a decent person. Your Honor let me love my son and do right by him!" Steve took his seat,

"Thank you, Mr. McDermott. In fact thank you all. The court will take a recess and return in thirty minutes with my decision."

During the break, Steve, his friends, and his attorney stood in the hallway. After approximately forty minutes the judge emerged into the courtroom with his determination.

Sitting up in his seat, the judge rendered his decision. "The court has taken into consideration all of the aggravating circumstances and mitigation in this matter, and after reviewing my notes of this hearing, affidavits submitted, and the penitentiary records and transcript from the trial over eight years ago. I did come across some things which troubled me greatly. However, it is this court's opinion that the child would be best served by having his father in his life. I believe that the success the child has had in school will only be enhanced by having the father as an active part of his life."

Sandra and Melanie started to sob.

"Therefore, this court will grant the motion and order one visit per week, five holidays per year, Christmas or Christmas eve, and visits on the day before the child's birthday."

"Mr. McDermott, I believe in you. I think you've learned your lesson but please know that any abuse of these privileges, or any further contact with the criminal justice system will result in the revocation of these parental rights. Do you understand Mr. McDermott?"

Steve wiped tears from his eyes "Yes I do!"

Sandra placed her head in the arms of her attorney, crying and sobbing. "This is wrong! This is a terrible mistake!"

"Mr. Daniels you would do well to advise your client about these conditions because if there is the slightest violation of any of them, this court will not hesitate to act with a strong and swift hand! Counsels, you can pick up the court orders from the clerk's office tomorrow after twelve O Clock. Mr. McDermott, you better make these papers your bible."

"Excuse me your honor."

"Yes Ms. Chase?"

"For the record, "With all due respect, we seriously object to the court's ruling and will do everything within our means to have this decision reversed."

The Judge never looked up. "Seek whatever further remedies you deem necessary, Ms. Chase. He slammed his gavel on the bench. "Court's adjourned!"

Steve whispered in his attorney's ear. Mr. Daniels rose from his seat and walked over to Ms. Chase. "Ms. Chase, may I have a brief word with you?"

"What is it, what do you want now Mr. Daniels? Haven't you and your client caused enough problems?"

"Funny Ms. Chase! My client would like to use some of the money raised by his defense fund to pay for Ms. Porter's legal expenses."

"Really!"

"Yes, that's what he told me to offer you. If you send me your bill, I'll forward it to him so that he can write the check."

"Hey, sounds good to me but, I'll discuss it with my client. That's mighty generous of your client Mr. Daniels! Wow, I guess maybe there is one good bone in his body. I guess I take back one of the negative things I said about him; only one."

On his way out of the building Steve's attorney gave a statement to one of the reporter. "Today we've seen a victory for the common man. My client took his case to the judicial system and we prevailed. This is a victory for all fathers who have been wronged or cheated out of precious, quality time with their children, time which they can never get back." Pointing to the camera, "Fathers, you, call me, I'll fight for your rights! Call **1**-800-DAD-FITE!"

"Mr. McDermott what do you have to say?

"I am very happy. My only desire today was to be granted the opportunity to be a father to my son and this court made that possible. Justice has been served because a father and his son were brought together. This court does have a heart.

CHAPTER 17

A few days later, across the street in front of Belvedere Elementary School Steve sat hoping to get a glimpse of Jason before he boarded the school bus for home however, to Steve's surprise Jason was sitting on the swings, playing with a model car and waiting for the bus to pull up. As the bus pulled up Jason jumped up and ran over to the bus holding the model car in his right hand. Steve followed the bus as it pulled off. After about one mile of traveling, the bus pulled over to the curb and Jason stepped off the bus. Jason was met by his mother at the curb, and escorted him into the house. Steve pulled off

ONE WEEK LATER

Steve was sitting in the Selections Restaurant with Sandra sitting across the restaurant frowning. Jason was escorted from across the room, by a court appointed social worker, to sit with Steve on their first father-son visit.

Steve occasionally sipped from a glass. "Hello Jason, how are you?"

Jason mumbled, "I'm Fine."

"Do you want anything to eat or drink?"

"No, sir, I already ate. My mom told me not to accept anything from strangers."

"Well, I know you don't know me, but I'm not a stranger I'm your father."

"Yeah, my mom talk to me about you."

"If it's okay with you, Jason, we're going to be spending time together getting to know one another." Jason nodded.

"Okay, now we can do a lot of fun things together, if that's okay with you?" Jason nodded again.

Steve removed from a bag a shiny blue Mustang model car. "Look, Jason, I brought this gift for you."

"Wow, thank you, Mr. McDermott!" He smiled.

"You know, Jason since we're going to be spending a lot of time together, why don't you start calling me Steve?"

"Okay" He played with the model car, never looking up.

"What do you like to do when you're not at school?"

"Sit in my backyard at home or play catch with my baseball and glove."

"Do you have a lot of toys at home?"

"Not really."

"Well we'll have to work on that. Maybe we can play catch soon?" Steve called the visit to a close. "Well, Jason, I think your mom is ready to go. I'm really happy she let us meet today. I'll see you next time, okay"

"Okay, thanks for the car, I really like it."

"My pleasure Jason."

Jason is escorted back over to where Sandra was waiting for him. Sandra takes Jason's arm and made her way to the door. Jason looked back and wave at Steve. Sandra absolutely refused to look back in Steve's direction.

A few days pass and Steve parked his pickup truck down the block from where Sandra lived. "She should be coming out any minute now."

Steve knew that Sandra's bakery: Bright Start Bakery opens at 7:00 AM. At 6:30 AM a school bus pulled up in front of the house and Jason ran out escorted by Sandra onto the bus.

"Have a great day at school honey."

"Okay mom."

Sandra waved goodbye. As the bus pulled off, down the street Sandra got in her vehicle and drove off headed in the opposite direction.

Steve pulled his truck in front of Sandra's house. Out of the bed of his truck he removed a lawnmower and began cutting the lawn. "I know this is all about impressing Jason but, I am really pushing the limits here." After finishing and sweeping up the grass trimmings Steve returned to his truck and removed a large box containing a backyard swing-set and assembled it.

Steve returned to the front seat of his truck and took out a new baseball and baseball glove. Placing them on the back porch of the house with a card that read, 'From Steve; your father.'

Noticing that the railing on the back porch had fallen he returned to his toolbox and quickly repaired the fallen railing. "I guess those carpentry workshops in prison are finally paying off."

That evening when Sandra and Jason arrived home, Jason jumped out of the vehicle. "Mom, look."

"Look at what?"

"Look at the swing set."

"Wow, I wonder where this came from and who cut the grass?"

Jason ran over to the porch, grabbed the ball, glove, and the card. "Mom, it's from my father; Steve."

Sandra stared in absolute disbelief. She hid her displeasure not wanting to damper Jason's joy. She mumbled, "Isn't this idiot full of surprises?" On Sandra's way into the house she noticed that the porch railing had been repaired. "A man of many talents I see. I should rip it off. I don't need any help from him. I wish he'd get that into his thick, sick skull."

Sandra sat her bags on the counter and grabbed a soda out of the refrigerator. Her mom entered through the back door. "The yard looks nice and, when did you buy the new swing set?"

"Jason's show-off want-to-be father is responsible for that."

"Oh that's interesting."

"You think so, Mom."

"Who are those letters from?"

"Steve the Rapist!"

"I thought you got rid of those?"

"Yeah, I started to but I decided to hold on to them. Now that it is obvious that he's going to be around Jason I think it's important that I get to know a little bit more about this manipulating monster."

Okay, well is there anything interesting in them."

"No, just a whole lot of I'm sorry, please forgive me."

"Well Sandra dear, do you think he's truly trying to gain your forgiveness?"

"Mom, he raped me and left me for dead! He also ruined my relationship with Adam, hell no, never! My how quick some people forgive and forget.

A few weeks went by and Steve was having another restaurant visit with Jason. This time Jason was a little more relaxed and open.

"Look, Jason, I got you another model car." Pulling the car out of a bag.

"Wow" Jason responded, "Thank you." My mom was really upset about you cutting the grass and doing the other stuff to help out around the house, but I really like the swing-set and I've been using my new baseball glove too."

"Hey, I have a brilliant idea. Maybe we can have our next visit at the park? I'll bring my glove and we can play catch, what do you think about that?"

"That would be awesome." He looked across the room. "Hey, Mom, can me and Steve meet and play catch at a park next time? Please can we, mom, please?"

"Jason, honey you should worry about this meeting and this meeting only. We will talk about everything else when we get home."

"Jason, your mom and I will work that out with the social worker. Here is my phone number. You can call me anytime if it's alright with your mom.

"All right, Steve, I'll see you later, Mom looks like she's really ready to go." Jason gets up from the table and walks over to his mom. The two of them along with the social worker walk out of the door.

On their way out Sandra glances back at Steve. "I don't like the fact that you came to my house you creep but, thanks for the toys and the repairs to the porch."

Steve smiles, "Just trying to be here for my son."

Sandra gives Steve another blank look. "Please keep all of your kind deeds directed toward Jason only! I'm still not happy about this whole dedicated daddy thing!"

"Understood Sandra."

"That's Ms. Porter to you!"

"Understood Ms.

CHAPTER 18

The beauty of a sunlit day made it the perfect day for spending time out at the ballpark. Waiting for Jason, Steve stood on the field tossing a baseball in the air at a little league diamond. Jason and Sandra arrived and Sandra takes a seat in the bleachers.

"Hey, Jay, you ready to play some catch?" Steve waved at Sandra but got no response. Jason was still acting a bit reserved but ran out onto the field and got ready to catch the ball.

Steve asked, "Jason, which one do you like best, throwing the ball or catching it?"

Shrugging his shoulders, he said, "I like both."

"Okay, I'll back up a little more and then, you throw the ball to me." Steve backed up about five feet. Steve threw Jason the ball and, Jason caught it. "All right Jason, let her rip! Jason throw the ball to Steve, "Wow Jason you've got a pretty strong arm."

After a short break the two continued playing. Sandra busied herself reading on her tablet. Steve threw Jason the ball and Jason attempted to chase it down. Jason stumbled and fell, slightly twisting his ankle. "Jason, honey, are you all right?"

Steve ran over to Jason. Getting there first, he picked Jason up and carried him back in the direction of where Sandra was approaching.

"Dammit, I knew this wasn't a good idea. He's just a kid you know!"

"Sandra trust me, he's fine. He only twisted his ankle a little bit he can walk that off."

"Trust you, really, really? I don't even like you! This isn't the major league, Jason, I told you to be careful. Come on, that's enough of this torture for the day."

"Mom I'm fine! I want to keep playing!"

Sandra took Jason from Steve and left the park. Steve shook his head and mumbled, "Women! This is going to be harder than I expected. No wonder she's in a bed by herself at night! If it were left up to her Jason would be a complete Wuss. Not going to happen to my son, Ms. Porter!"

A week later Steve phoned Sandra's home. Jason answered. "Jason, this is Steve. How are you?"

"I'm doing good. Can we go back to the park to play catch soon?"

"That's why I'm calling. My job is participating in a junior League tournament and tryouts for the team is in two weeks. I think you should tryout. What do you think about that?"

"Wow, can I please tryout?"

"Check with your mom and let me know."

Jason shouted into the kitchen "Hey, mom, Steve's job is starting a team for kids. Mom, please can I tryout?" Its at Steve's job. Can I be on the team?

"Jay you are really trying my patience. Okay you can be on the team."

He shouted, "She said yes, when do we start?"

"We start tryouts in a few weeks."

Two afternoons a week, Steve met Jason and Sandra at the park to practice. On the morning of the tryouts, Steve showed up early to the house to pick up Jason. "Come on, Jay, we should get there a little early in order to get some practice in before tryouts starts."

As Steve got back into his car he said to Sandra, "I can give you a ride to the game too if you like?"

"That's okay, I do have a car you know, creep. I will meet you'll there!"

At the park, Jason had done a pretty good job, catching balls and hitting pitches. Jason came up to bat but missed the first and second pitch by a mile. On the third pitch Jason hit the ball and it soared out of the park.

"It's a homerun. Homerun, homerun!" Sandra shouted from her seat.

Steve shouted, "Good job Jay. Way to go slugger." Sandra jumped up in joyous celebration.

Jason rounded the bases running as fast as he could. Jason's team won as a result of his homerun. The team coach met Jason in the dugout and said, "Great hit, Jason, welcome to the team!"

The coach suggested that all the team members go out to the local restaurant to celebrate and, to get their jerseys. The parents agreed and they all met at the local Steak and Shake.

One of the moms congratulated Jason on his game-winning homerun. She turned to Steve and said, "I see where your son gets his good looks from!" She handed Steve her phone number. "Give me a call."

After a hour of celebrating, Sandra prepared to head home. Steve politely walked Jason and Sandra to their vehicle. Steve gave Jason a congratulatory high five and waved goodbye.

Steve told Sandra, "Hey, Sandra, thanks for letting Jason be a part of the team. I think he'll do very well."

"Jason, its time to go, get in the car."

"I know that this is really difficult for you, it's difficult for me as well. I'm really not that bad of a guy." He turned to Jason; "Okay, Jay, I'll talk to you soon."

"Steve, you can save that for the other moms who appear swooned by your looks. Make sure you use that phone number she gave you. Maybe she can be your next victim?"

Walking back to his car, Steve heard Sandra trying to start her vehicle, but to no avail. Sandra continued trying to start the vehicle, but after a few more attempts the vehicle would not start. Steve motioned for Jason to let down his window.

"Doesn't sound like it wants to start? Let me give you guys a ride home and I'll have the car towed to an auto shop in the morning?"

"No, it will start, we're okay. It always does this. I'll wait a minute and try it again. Thank but no thanks!" Sandra continued trying but still had no success.

"I don't think you should do that, it already sounds like you've flooded the engine."

"I'll call my friend Melanie and, she'll come and pick us up. You can go! Just leave we're good."

"Really, Sandra it's not a big deal. I can run you guys home, it's really not a problem."

"Mom, why can't we ride with Steve?"

"No, we can wait on Melanie!"

"Mom, Steve is already here we can ride with him?"

"Well, Jason, if you insist."

Jason smiled, jumped out of the car, and got into the back seat of Steve's vehicle, leaving the front seat for Sandra. "Mom you sit in the front seat."

"Oh my, how thoughtful of you."

Steve opened the front door for Sandra.

"Thanks, I can get my own door, thank you."

During the ride home Jason and Steve talked about the tryouts and the team practice schedule. "Jay, you really did well out there on the field."

"Did you see how far I hit that ball?"

"Yes, didn't you see your mom and I jumping for joy?"

"When I came around home plate everybody was jumping and shouting, run, run!"

Sandra responded, "Okay, Jason, get a grip. OMG."

"It was good to see you having fun. Your happiness is important to me Jay!"

The car pulled into the driveway of the house and stopped. Sandra jumped out. She looked over at Steve and said, "Thank you."

Steve smiled and says, "Can I get your car towed in the morning?"

"No, I will handle that through my motor club."

"See you later, slugger. Talk to you soon."

"Ok, dad, can you pick me up for practice on Saturday morning?"

Steve smiled and, with tears welling up in his eyes said, "You know it, son."

As Sandra and Jason entered into the living room Sandra asked, "Mother what in the world are you smiling about?

"Well, I was just thinking about how good it is that things have turned around for you and Jason, that's all."

"Now mom don't you read anything into this, it was just a innocent ride from a Jason's father."

"Truthfully Sandra, Steve really does seem to care a lot for Jason and, that's a good thing right?"

"Well mom he is only around because of Jason. Thanks to the Judge I've just got to deal with it."

"Well Sandra since we're talking what about somebody in your life?" Sandra is shocked!

"Mom, I know what you're thinking but the idea sounds absolutely and ridiculously crazy! You can't go from rape to romance!"

"Me and Steve, how crazy does that sound?"

CHAPTER 19

About six months later Sandra and Melanie were enjoying an evening a restaurant catching up.

"Sandra, you look like a breath of fresh air."

Smiling, she responded, "Oh do I, maybe it's a result of me getting back into church?"

"How are things going with Jason and Mr. Dedicated Daddy Steve?" The two laughed.

"Well, life is all right. It's been over a year and a half since Steve's been in Jason's life and Jason loves it. They spend time a couple of days during the month hanging out. Some mornings Steve shows up and takes Jason to school or some days he will pick him up from school. They have a pretty good relationship. Of course, that has nothing to do with me. That's just between the two of them. I'm a little bit better since I was unable to do anything to prevent it."

"And by the way, why is everybody worried about Steve? Steve is a part of Jason's life and that's all. No one is concerned about me and how I'm doing?"

"Sandra, I'm sorry, I didn't mean it like that. I was just making conversation. You know I'm concerned about you and Jason! But I must admit, there is something different about you!"

"I'm just saying, Mel, can't we talk about me without talking about Steve?"

"I see his presence still bothers you."

"It's not really a bother but Steve seems to be the topic of everyone's conversation. My mom keeps making relationship suggestions. She laughed. "Can you imagine that?"

"Well now Sandra, he is hot and with a few minor adjustments I can see why someone would suggest that."

"Now, here you go. Does anybody remember what this man did to me? I don't know if I will ever be able to get pass that! They say, time heals all wounds but this wound is quite deep"

"Girl, you're right, but you must admit Steve did tone up some while he was locked up and his body is quite interesting; 1-800-Hot-Body."

"Mel you are killing me. Maybe, you should hook up with him?"

"That's a good idea. Can I get his number from you? I'm just joking girl." The two laughed.

"Okay, Melanie, okay, I will admit I have noticed that he is somewhat attractive, but I think its more the way he treats Jason above his looks."

"See, I knew your weren't blind San, you can still spot a handsome man when you see one! I do think it's awesome that he is so into his son; that's extremely rare these days. Not to mention as I remember from the porch he repaired, he really does knows how to swing a hammer and drive a nail. And did I mention that He is show-nuff fine?"

"Mel, I'm really not all that interested in what he's swinging. How do you say it, been there done that!" The two laughed.

"Okay, so how's business at the bakery?"

"Business is good. Since Jason has someone to occupy his time I'm thinking about finally opening up that second location I've always talked about."

"That's awesome! I told you things would turn around for you. And oh yeah Sandra girl, did I mention how fine he is."

"Melanie you are a trip. Girl, the pickings are extremely slim out there. I went out with an attractive guy who comes in the bakery every morning. Turns out he had a thing for my Counter clerk and wanted me to hook the two of them up. The Counter clerk is happily married with two kids but when I told the clerk about it he wanted the guys number and said that he wants to accept his invitation."

"OMG, you've got to be kidding."

"No, Mel, I was outdone. The others I tried to date were either too much into themselves, married, homosexual, looking for someone to take care of them, or just looking for a side-piece."

"I know what you mean Sandra."

"This has really been fun. Jason's team has a game today. I better get going before I miss it."

At the park Jason was out on the field playing second base. The ball was hit into leftfield. They threw the ball to Jason. As Jason was reaching to tag the runner out their legs got tangled and both players fell to the ground in pain.

The coaches, other players, and Steve ran to them. Jason exclaimed, "Coach, I'm fine, let me walk it off."

The player on the opposite team seemed to be okay and in no real need of medical attention.

"However, Jason said, "Dad, my leg hurts really bad."

Steve carried Jason to the car. He placed Jason across the back seat and sped off to the nearest hospital.

"Hey, slugger how you feeling back there?"

"My leg really hurts dad."

"The doctor will check it out and, I'm sure he'll give you something for the pain."

Once Steve arrived they took a seat waiting in the lobby for an examining room to open up. Steve stepped out into the lobby to use his cell phone.

"Hey, Sandra, this is Steve. Everything is fine. Jason and I are at the emergency room at Metropolitan Hospital Center. Jason banged his leg in the game with another player but he's a tough kid. We're waiting for the doctor to call us in and examine him."

"Okay, I'm on my way there right now." Sandra hung up the phone. "Mel, Jason got injured in the game. They're at the emergency room. I got to get over there." Sandra Left.

Sometime later, the nurse came out to the lobby and called out Jason's name.

Steve responded, "Here he is over here nurse."

"Are you the boy's father?"

"Yes, I am."

"Okay, I see where he gets his good looks from. We will get your son into the examining room now so that the doctor can see him. You can come in with him or you can stay out here with me whichever you prefer."

Steve chose to go into the examining room with Jason. A short time later Sandra arrived to the hospital. "Excuse me officer, I'm here to see my son Jason Porter who was brought in a while ago. Can you tell me which room he's in?"

"Hold on miss let me check the list. Okay miss go down this hall to examining room number eight your family is in there with the doctor."

When Sandra walked into the room she said, "Honey, how are you?"

"Hi Mom, my leg really hurts."

"Oh, this must be your wife?"

"No, doctor I'm, his mother."

Steve joked, "That's okay, Doc, we get that all the time."

"My apologies. Well mom Jason's leg is not broke just pretty badly banged up. I'll give you a prescription for some pain medication. All the directions for use will be with the medication. Mom do you have any questions?"

"How long should he stay off his leg?"

"He will have to take it easy for a couple of weeks."

"Father do you have any questions?"

"No doctor, I don't."

"What about you Jason do you have any questions?

"Yes, when will the pain stop and when can I play baseball again?"

"No baseball activities Jason, for at least two weeks."

"I'm sorry doctor, I do have one question. Will he need a crutch or a cast to limit the movement of his leg?"

"Yes Mr. McDermott. I'll tell the nurse to get you a pair of crutches. He can use them for the next few days. He should also avoid stairs as much as possible. Stay off that leg slugger."

The nurse returned with the discharge papers for Jason. She said, "Mr. and Mrs. Porter, you can pick up the prescription at your local pharmacy."

Sandra responds, "Whatever."

Steve and Sandra looked at each other and gave a sarcastic stare. Steve placed Jason in a wheelchair and rolled him to the car placing him in the back seat.

Arriving home Sandra held the door open. Sandra allowed Steve to carry Jason to his room and help prepare him for bed.

After Jason is bedded down, Steve came down the stairs. "This is a nice place you have, Sandra."

"Thanks, it's not much but it's ours.

"I'll call the coach and let him know how Jay is doing, I hope he's able to get some sleep tonight".

"Yes it's been an eventful day for my child but, hopefully the medication he took will help"

"So, in the words of the nurse and doctor, how are you Mrs. Porter?"

"Funny, I see you got jokes, Mr. McDermott. Thanks for getting him settled in. Jay will call you tomorrow. Have a good night Steve."

"Sandra, Can I have a brief moment of your time?

"I've had a full day but if you insist."

"Sandra, I know that this is really awkward but please just give me thirty second to finally get this off of my chest."

"Okay, two minutes."

Steve rested on the edge of sofa chair. "All kidding aside, Sandra, I know that this hasn't been easy for you. I did something very terrible and I am truly, truly sorry. I wish that it wouldn't have ever happened. I've spent many days wishing I could," (he wiped tears from his eyes), "change what happened on that terrible night. Please, if you can find it in your heart please except my sincere apology. I was going through a lot and the alcohol didn't make things any better. You are too good of a woman and a mother to be put through what I put you through. I hope one day with God's help, you will be able to forgive me for my mistakes. I was taught that respect is something you earn and my goal is to earn back the respect I lost through my past mistake. My life seems to be back on track. I like my job, I've satisfied all of the conditions of my early release, and Jason is the son I've always wanted. Okay, that's all I wanted to say."

Sandra handed Steve some tissue. "Well, Steve, I'm not making any promises but I must admit you've been good for Jason and he really enjoys having a father in his life."

"I feel the same way and it is good to be in my son's life."

"Steve, I will admit that I had to do a lot of praying and I've come a long, long, long way from where I was over a year ago. Jason has always dreamed of playing baseball on a team and now he's playing in his second season; he's happy and, I like it when he's happy."

"Yeah, I agree, he'll probably make team captain this year. "

"Having you in his life has made him a lot happier. With the bakery and all of its demands on me I was really starting to worry about Jason. God does work in mysterious ways and prayer really does still work. Many people would be terribly shocked to hear me say this but; I do accept your apology. Of course, with the understanding, this is only about Jason and nothing else?"

Steve responded, "Of course."

"Speaking of worrying, no disrespect, but Sandra, who's worried about you?"

Sandra looked at Steve with a blank stare

Wow, I didn't see that one coming. You sound just like my friend Melanie. Aren't you being a little nosy, Mr. McDermott? The truth is if you must know, I've been extremely busy trying to make things right for Jason and make things right at the bakery, I really haven't had time for me but I'm doing just fine."

"Well, you know what they say, all work and no play makes Sandra a very unhappy girl."

"No worries handyman, I'm just fine."

"Okay, just checking."

"How ironic is this that I'm sitting on a couch being counseled by the guy who raped me? You know," pointing at Steve, "If I'd listen to some people, I would let you worry about me."

"Well, in as much as I am the one involved in causing you pain I would love to help you get rid of your pain.

"For some reason, you are attracting a pretty good following among my family and friends."

"Well maybe that's not a bad idea?

Sandra laughed. "Real funny, Mr. funny-man. Don't forget our agreement, it's all about Jason."

"I tell you what, Sandra, how about dinner?"

"What do you mean dinner?"

"Let me take you out to dinner this weekend."

"I told you, Steve; no promises."

"I don't know. I'm still uncomfortable with this whole thing."

"Come on, it's just dinner nothing else. Just two people out to dinner eating, that's all!"

"Well, let me think about it and I'll let you know."

"I'll settle for that."

"If we need to, we can take Jason with us?"

"Just dinner, no strings attached, right, Steve?"

"Right, unless you say different."

"Wow, the jokes just keep coming don't they."

"I'm sorry but, we should try to at least be comfortable around each other for Jason's sake?"

"Okay, I hope I'm not making a terrible mistake. And just in case I am, we'll leave Jason out of this event."

Steve got up off the couch and made his way to the door. Sandra walked behind him to lock the door. Steve turned and accidently brushed up against her. Sandra stood still. Steve placed his arms around her and Sandra gave in to Steve's warm embrace. Sandra pulled away and Sandra pushed Steve toward the door.

"Good night, Steve."

"Good night Sandra."

After shutting the door Sandra said, "Why did I let him take me there? God give me strength because, this four year commitment to celibacy is quickly coming unglued."

As he sat in the front seat of his car Steve said, "Wow I knew she was a good kisser! I think I'm in love with the same woman that sent me to prison."

"Now where are those keys? OMG. Don't tell me I left my keys in there. Steve went back and knocked on the front door. Sandra was startled.

"What in the world! What do you want now Steve?"

"I came back for another kiss."

"You've got to be kidding me. I know I would come to regret opening up to you."

"No Sandra really I left my keys somewhere in there."

"That's a lame excuse Steve. Just leave and be on your way. That's what I get for trying to trust you!"

"No Sandra Really, I'm not being deceptive I left my keys on the end of the table."

"Steve you should really stop playing like this. This is hard enough for all of us without the little added comedy."

"I'm sorry Sandra. My mistake."

Sandra unlocked the door. "Here is your keys funny man. Goodnight."

"What, no good night kiss?"

"Goodnight Jason's father!"

CHAPTER 20

A week later, Sandra and Steve were sitting at a table in a seafood restaurant. On the table sat a dozen of freshly cut roses packaged to perfection and, a box of assorted chocolates wrapped in colorful paper sealed with a bow. The two laughed as they discussed a disgruntled customer who visited the bakery earlier that day.

"People can be so demanding. The woman wanted us to bake another pan of lemon Danishes ten minutes before closing time. Now, I'm all for customer satisfaction but what would we do with the other eleven Danishes?

"Do you deal with situations like that on a daily basis?"

"No. Most days run smoothly and the majority of customers don't give us any problems.

"How are things going where you work, Mr. McDermott?"

"Well, business is good. I can see building a future with this engineering company. They're talking about making me a Regional Manager."

Sandra nodded. "That's sounds good."

"Weren't you talking about opening up another location for the bakery?"

"Wow, Mr. McDermott have you been ease dropping on some of my conversations.

"No, Jason mentioned it some time ago."

"Oh did he?"

Steve nodded, "Yes he did."

"So, tell me Steve what else did Jason mention to you."

"Since you ask, he also mentioned that you haven't went out on a date in a long time."

Folding her arms, "Oh did he? Wait until I talk to him." Steve laughed.

"Your timing is magnificent Mr. waiter. You couldn't have come at a better time. Okay, I'll have the Tilapia with lemon sauce, a baked potato and some asparagus on the side."

"Alright sir."

"Maam, what will you be having?"

"I'll have the tilapia with lemon sauce; a baked potato and broccoli. Oh, and, can I have a glass of white wine as well?"

The waiter closed his ordering case. "I'll be back in a minute with your drinks. Sir, would you like anything to drink?"

"No, just some more water."

"Are you sure sir I can get you whatever you need?"

"No just some water." After the waiter walked away Steve said, "This is a nice restaurant. I haven't been here in years."

Sandra joked, "I wonder why?" They laughed,

"Oh, now you're the one with jokes! I'm glad you're feeling a little bit more relaxed."

"Now, Steve, back to you and Jason who evidently, can't hold water."

Steve smiled. "What are you talking about? It was just innocent conversation that's all."

In walked Steve's ex-boss. Passing by the table he stopped "Steve McDermott, is that you?"

Steve stood to shake his hand. "Mr. Scott it's good to see you. And by the way, thanks for the referral. The job is working out very well."

"Glad it's working out for you."

"Oh, I'm sorry. Mr. Scott, this is Sandra a friend of mine!"

"Hello, you look so familiar. Have we met before?"

"I don't think so."

"Oh, well, Steve, you two have a great evening, we'll talk soon. Call me if I can help you with anything else. Nice meeting you Sandra."

After Mr. Scott left Sandra said, "This Tilapia is very tasty."

"I'm glad you're enjoying the dinner. I'm really enjoying being out with you tonight. I couldn't think of anyone who I would rather be out with other than you."

"From what I've seen and from what Jason tells me, you have your share of women standing in line. Who else are you buying nice things for?"

"I've been out with a few interesting individuals but that's all, just being nice. Now this is a welcome change to what I've experienced over the last year."

Placing her fork on her plate she said, "Thank God we're just friends and they're no strings attached, right?"

"I know, I'm just letting you know that I'm enjoying your company."

"I will admit that I am enjoying your company as well, and thanks again for the gifts. However, I've got to take it easy on the dinner wine, I'm really starting to feel it. It's been a long time since I've been out on a dinner date like this. I never saw this day coming but I believe I'm okay with it now."

"What time was your mom getting Jason back home?"

"He is probably at home and the two of them, crutches and all, are probably tucked away in bed by now. Oh, but don't worry, I'll have a talk with Jason in the morning about discussing our business.

Steve shook his head. "Me and my son were just having innocent conversation that's all!"

"I know, that's all he and I will have in the morning is innocent conversation, that's all!"

"Oh, yeah, he also asked me why his mother and dad couldn't live in the same house like other families?"

"Did he really?"

"Yes, he did!"

"Well, what did you tell him?"

"I told him that many years ago I made a terrible mistake, which really hurt his mom and that I'm praying that one day she will be able to forgive me and rest assured, I didn't tell him what the mistake was."

Sandra put her head down in embarrassment, stating; "You just wait until I talk to that child of mine. We're going to have a long talk."

The two shared another laugh as they continued eating and drinking.

When Sandra got up to go to the restroom, she stumbled slightly but braced herself on the edge of the table.

"Are you alright?"

"Yes Steve, I'm fine, just a little too much dinner wine. Were you trying to get me drunk or something?" Steve took offense but hid it well.

"Really, I would never do that to you or anyone else. Even though you may not believe me, I really care about you and want to make you happy. Not just because of my son but because I've caused you enough pain and I think you're incredibly special!"

Sandra blushed while still maintaining her balance. "I know, I was just joking and I've also decided that you're a decent guy too. Let's just keep it in the moment."

"I'm good with that." Cool, then Sandra, you shouldn't mind me being your designated driver."

"I'm fine but just to be safe, okay. What about my car?"

"Don't worry, I can pick it up tomorrow morning, if that's alright with you.

"Okay, that sounds like a good plan. I'll be right back."

While Sandra was in the restroom Steve glanced across the room and noticed his ex-wife Jennifer working as a manager in the restaurant. He walked over to where she was working.

"Hello Jennifer."

"Steve. Wow. Look at you. How are things going?"

"Things are good. Just working and taking it one day at a time."

"Well maybe we can get together and catch up on old times?"

"How are you and your spouse Kelly doing?"

"That phrase in my life ended a few years ago, thankfully."

"So Steve lets make a date?"

"I don't think so. I'm really not interested. But it is good seeing you. Take care and tell Kelly Steve said, get a life!"

When Sandra returned to the table Steve paid the bill and pulled his car around to the door. Steve was waiting ready to escort Sandra to the car. Steve opened the passenger door and helped Sandra into the front seat.

On the ride home, Sandra relaxed, as she enjoyed the music.

"Was that another one of your female fans you were talking to in the restaurant?"

"No, just an old associate who means nothing at all to me. But can you get rid of this phone number the waiter called himself slipping me on the down low. Definitely not interested in any of that."

"Are you sure? People are so bold today!"

"I know, right? I guess sooner or later we'll talk about that kiss the other afternoon?"

"What kiss Steve? I don't know anything about a kiss the other afternoon at the front door of my home."

"Wow, you must moonlight as a comedian or something?"

"What is there to talk about? Did you have a problem with it?"

"No, I enjoyed it immensely.

"All of this kindness, all the gifts that you've been given me, I'm not use to, and that cologne, OMG, that cologne!"

At Sandra's home, the lights were out and everyone appeared to be asleep. Steve walked Sandra to the door. "Sandra, are you going to be alright?"

"I'll be fine if I can just find my keys. Here they are." Sandra opened the door and slowly turned requesting a hug from Steve.

"Wow, this must be the nightcap or something?"

"What, are you complaining again, Steve?

"Oh no! Any attention I get from you is golden." Steve gave Sandra a quick hug. As Steve removed his hand from around Sandra's waist, Sandra gripped him tighter and the two exchanged another passionate kiss.

"Let me get you in the house, I think you've had a little too much to drink." Steve took Sandra by the arm.

Sandra responded, "No Steve, I'm completely aware of what's I'm doing. You asked me to forgive you and I need to show you that I have. I've been fighting this feeling but I don't want to fight it any longer. Everyone else sees it and now I do too. I've never had anyone to care for me and be concerned about me like you do. I think your good for Jason and me both."

Sandra pulled him into the house. They ended up on the downstairs couch. Looking into Steve's eyes, she unbuttoned his shirt and ran her fingers through his hair. "Steve, I can't fight this anymore. I know this is going to sound crazy but please make love to me. Please be gentle!"

"Sandra, you don't know how long I've wanted to kiss every part of your body. Everything in me wants to caress you and make you feel good for as long as you'll let me. Are you sure this is you talking and not the wine?"

"No, this is my passion talking, I need you! Make love to me now and, we'll make sense of all this later."

The two continued kissing. Steve picked up Sandra and carried her into her bedroom. Steve placed her on the bed. "Are you sure this is alright. I don't ever want to hurt you again?"

Steve locked the door. Sandra removed Steve's shirt and slowly unzipped his pleated slacks. Steve removed Sandra's blouse and slowly unsnapped the front of her bra, unleashing what he had only dreamed about kissing and caressing.

Sandra rubbed her hand softly across Steve's well-carved chest and placed her lips upon it. The tips of Steve's finger slowly moved down Sandra's spine. Steve whispered into Sandra's ear, "I am so sorry and I will never hurt you again!"

Sandra whispered, "I know, make love to me!"

As the two exchanged passionate kisses their clothes were completely removed and tossed to the floor.

As Steve inserted his phallus into Sandra, she moaned slightly but her moans quickly turn into muffled screams of, "Yes, Yes," because of the pillow she pulled up to cover her mouth. Steve made love to her whole body, causing every inch of her to scream from within. Sandra's sexual needs were thoroughly satisfied.

The two passed the night caressing each other and methodically fulfilling each other's needs. Their built-up passions were completely emptied, as the night grew closer to morn.

"I should leave, Sandra?"

"I don't want you to but if you think that's best?" Sandra gripped onto Steve tightly. I don't know if everyone, especially Jason, is ready for this but I know I am!"

"Okay, I better get going? Steve slipped out the house quietly just before daybreak, unnoticed.

CHAPTER 21

Several weeks later Sandra, her mom, and Melanie were lounging in the backyard of Sandra's house. They were listening to music and discussing business at the bakery and what was going on in each other's life.

"So, Sandra, how is things at the bakery," Melanie asked.

"Things are going very well, the planning for the second location is underway. It's looking more and more like a reality. How are things with you and that hot guy you met at the cleaners?"

"Funny you should mention him, San." She swallowed a sip of her drink. "He's been constantly emailing me about going out but I'm getting bad vibes about him."

Sandra responded, "What are you talking about. He sounds like a good catch for you?"

"Look who's talking, Missy-Ann!" Sandra's mom offered a comical smirk.

Steve came walking into the backyard, returning with Jason after spending the day with him. "Speaking of good catches, there's yours and oh my God, he is still fine." Melanie raised her glass as a toast.

The three of them broke out in restrained laughter. Sandra's mom rises from her seat and enters into the backdoor of the house. Melanie said, "Sandra, I'm your friend and I certainly wouldn't tell you anything wrong. Let go of the past! Everyone can see he wants to be a family with you and Jay. Life is too short and you've been through too much. I know it's easier said than done, but love does cover a multitude of faults. It does appear that he made a terrible mistake and he's paid for that mistake. I think he's good for you and Jay."

"I appreciate that and I have been giving a whole lot of thought to it." I must admit I do find it attractive the way he loves and cares for his son.

"Hello, Melanie, how's everybody, Steve asked?"

Melanie lowered her voice. "We're a lot better now that you're here."

Steve responds, "Okay that's a little awkward!"

Sandra's mom returned with glasses filled with lemonade and wearing a large grin. "Melanie, did you see how Sandra perked up when Steve walked in? You know all that stress you've built up working at the bakery I bet a massage would probably do you good and, Steve looks like he has strong hands."

Melanie added, "That sounds like a good idea to me! I mean San, you do need someone to massage your feet after a long day at the bakery."

"I know that's right! However, me and Steve are just friends!"

"I don't know, Mel, Sandra are you sure that's all?"

"That's all, Mom!"

"You know mother always knows best? I heard your office was full of roses one day last week."

"OMG, Sandra I can't believe you're withholding information for your friends?"

"Okay I have a secret admirer that's all!"

Steve said, "Excuse me Sandra, I'm going to get my tool bag I left the other day out of the basement?"

Melanie smirked, "Tools in the basement, what's that about, girl?"

"Well, he's been coming by the house occasionally working on some things."

"Yeah, I bet he's been working on some things alright!

"You know what, pointing at Melanie. If there were something between Steve and I surely, I wouldn't tell you two. Let me just say, it's funny but, Steve and I have grown closer than we once were. I've managed to forgive him for what he did to me." I needed to break free from the prison of my painful past and search for a brighter future.

Melanie shouted, "YES, YES, that's what I'm talking about."

The ladies enjoyed the rhythmic sounds of singer Robin Thick and, Blurred Lines. "*If you can't hear, what I'm try-na say, If you can't read, from the same page, Maybe I'm going deaf, Maybe I'm going blind, Maybe I'm out of my mind. OK, now he was close, Tried to domesticate you, But you're an animal, Baby, it's in your nature, Just let me liberate you, You don't need no papers, And that's why I'm gon' take you Good girl! I know you want it. I know you want it. I know you want it. You're a good girl! Can't let it get past me, me fall from plastic. Talk about getting blasted; I hate these blurred lines.................! Girl, their playing my song;...I know you want it. You're a good girl!*

Melanie jumped up out of her chair dancing, holding her glass in her hand, laughing.

Sandra's mother looks over at Sandra, "Melanie, She does have a new glow about her. God is good! You know what they say, don't you; God works in mysterious ways, Hallehhuh!"

"Watch out Melanie Mom's preaching again." Melanie laughed.

"I must admit Mel, Steve has turned out to be a pretty decent guy."

"Oh, now, he's STEVE? Wow, what a change?"

"You know what, I will never be able to figure you two out. I guess Steve is growing on all of us!"

The women laughed as they continued enjoying the music.

CHAPTER 22

Some months later Steve and Jason entered the house, returning from Jason's baseball game.

"Mom, you should have seen me, it was awesome! I hit the winning homerun." He raised both arms. Tears welled in her eyes.

"Mom, after the game the coach told me that he chose me to be on the All Star Team! I need to start practicing to get ready for the All Star game."

"Well, you better get some good rest. You're going to need your energy. Right?"

Steve escorted Jason to his room, bedded him down and shut the door behind him. "Good night, son."

"Good night, Dad, see you tomorrow."

Steve came into the living room. "You should have seen him. He played a really good game. Four for four in hits and he tagged a man out at second base." Steve leaned over and kissed Sandra on her left cheek. "By the way, have I told you lately how beautiful your are?"

Sandra just smiled. "What's wrong, you seem a little distant? Was it a rough day at the bakery? If you want me to make it all better I will?"

"No". She shook her head. "Nothings wrong, I've just got a lot on my mind and I guess. Sometimes I have to pause and really think about what's happening." But it feels good.

Just then the phone rang. "Hello. Oh, hi Adam." She turned slightly to avoid Steve overhearing her conversation. "How are things going, it's been a long time?"

"Things are great on my end! How are things with you and your son?"

"Things are going well for us, thanks for asking."

"Hey, I've really missed you, Sandra."

"I've missed you as well."

"I'm going to be in town and I would love to see you!"

"Okay, Adam, we'll see about that. When are you here?"

"I'm coming in on this Friday and leaving on Sunday."

Steve stepped into the kitchen.

"Are you coming to town for business or for pleasure?"

Adam laughed. "It's business but I really would like to hang out with you if you're available?"

Steve walked back into the room with a drink from the refrigerator and took a seat on the couch.

"Adam, it's good hearing from you but I'm in a relationship and things are good. It was good talking to you. Take care of yourself." Sandra hung up the phone.

"Wow, is that what's making you hesitant about our relationship Sandra? Maybe I should just leave?"

"I apologize, he's just an old friend who meant something to me at one time, but that was then you are now!"

Steve smiled. Sandra hugged Steve. He loosened up and the two shared a kiss.

Sandra said to Steve, "I need you to make love to me again, as she kissed Steve on both sides of his neck. "No one has ever made me feel like you make me feel." Sandra placed her lips on Steve's chest. "Steve, I haven't exploded like that in a very, very long time."

"Should I stay for a while? As Steve lowered Sandra blouse and began running his fingers through her hair. "I know it's going to be a shocker to some but; I think we should work on making things official."

Sandra looked into Steve's eyes intently. "I don't ever want to hurt again. Please promise to love me and be there for our son."

Kissing Sandra on her lips Steve replied; "If you promise to always look this sexy and always love me I'm all in!"

Sandra cut off the lights in the living room and walked down the hall and into the bedroom. She pushed Steve on the bed and slowly unbuckled his belt. After their clothes were removed the two slowly caressed each other's body. Steve kissed Sandra, starting with the top of her forehead and slowly descends all the way down; sending Sandra into a fit of passion.

"You are so beautiful, Sandra."

Sandra attempted to slow him down but the passion caused her to relax and let Steve's affection have free course.

Steve said, "Just relax and let me love every inch of you."

"Sandra kissed Steve. Steve was left paralyzed by passion and speechless, with the exception of a variety of passionate sounds which proved of Steve's sexual satisfaction.

"Steve, I'm falling in love with you." The two enjoyed sex in a variety of different positions. After a while Sandra ended up on top of Steve and the two inadvertently rolled off of the bed, landing on the carpeted floor.

The two laughed, "You know, Sandra, I wondered if I would ever be able to love again. I thank God everyday for you and Jay."

"Steve, God has truly made this possible. I love the way you love us. We need happiness and through you God has given that to us. I'm thanking Him too everyday for our new found joy."

"You and Jason's happiness are priority to me. Thank you Sandra for trusting me and giving me a chance at happiness as well. God is good!"

CHAPTER 23

ONE MONTH LATER

Steve pulled his pickup truck into the driveway and walked through the back door. As he entered the kitchen, he called out for Sandra.

Jason ran from around the corner and gave Steve a hug.

"Hey, slugger, how did you sleep?

"Good. Dad, I'm ready for the game today!"

"Jay, where's mom?"

"I think mom is in her room getting ready to go."

Steve walked down the hall calling Sandra's name. Eventually he came upon the bathroom door where Sandra was standing over the sink with a pregnancy test stick in her hand.

"Hey!" He paused. I was looking for you. What's going on?

The two looked at each other in shock and both gazes were drawn to the stick, which indicated a Positive sign. Steve kissed Sandra on the forehead and embraced her with a comforting hug.

"Hey, looks like I'm going to be a father again?"

"Yeah, looks like that's the case!"

7 MONTHS LATER

Sandra was lying in the hospital bed, Melanie was relaxing in a chair next to the bed, and the nurse was standing in the room turning the pages of Sandra's chart. Cradled in Sandra's arms was her newborn daughter.

"San, I still haven't figured out why you didn't name her after your best friend in the world, but I guess Maleah is close enough."

Doctor Montara walked into the room. The nurse received the baby out of Sandra's hands. "Come on, Maleah, it's time for a quick bath."

The Doctor flipped through Sandra's chart. "Okay, Ms. Porter, everything is great, you two have a beautiful, fully functioning baby girl. All of her vitals look great. Her respiratory tests are all normal, and her vision test look fine as well. I noticed the blood-type request form on the chart of your first child Jason, and just in case you were interested in knowing the blood type of your daughter, it's type O. The blood type of your son Jason's, according to our records is type A. Therefore you have a Type A and a Type O. Good combination."

Sandra was shocked. She sat up in the bed and interrupted the doctor, "No doctor Jason's blood type is type AB; I distinctly remember that."

The doctor responded; "It appears the record clerk made a mistake originally when your son was born and because you had already been discharged the staff was suppose to contact you concerning that mistake. But, it appears from your response today that no one contacted you with that correction?

"No they didn't."

"I'm glad we were able to finally clear that up. I hope that there were no major inconveniences?"

During the custody hearing her, attorney, Ms. Chase, checked the original birth records and saw that Steve's blood type was **Type AB**. The court didn't demand its own test because it didn't determine it as being necessary since paternity, wasn't an issue for debate. This can't be correct because that would mean..........OMG, this can't be." Her tears started to flow uncontrollably.

Sandra placed her head back and gazed toward the ceiling. "Is everything all right, Ms. Porter? You look puzzled and upset?

"No, Doctor, everything is okay. These are just tears of joy." She wiped her tears as she attempted to hide her emotional panic.

Placing his hand on her right shoulder, the doctor said, "You get some rest today and if everything maintains its course you'll be released tomorrow." Turning toward the door the doctor waved. "Thank you for all your help too Melanie."

Fighting back tears, Sandra mumbled, "Thank you, Doctor."

Sandra could hardly lay back and rest. "Her blood type is type O, and Steve's blood type is type B, which proves his fatherhood of Maleah but, Steve's fatherhood of Jason whose blood type is now A, is medically impossible. Oh my God, Melanie." She put both hands up to her cheek. "There's been another terrible mistake!"

"What in the world is going on now, San?"

"Steve can't possibly be Jason's biological father! Oh my God what am I going to do now? This is awful!"

Just then Steve and Jason walked through the door. Steve said, "Hello, ladies. Hey, what's with those sad faces? Is everything alright?"

"Honey, sit down. We've got to talk! There's been a terrible mistake!"

THE END.

MISTAKES

Also available are Ronnie's exciting relationship books guaranteed to propel you and your relationship to a happier and healthier place. Find love and keep it. These tools can equip you with what you need to enjoy the rest of life alongside the love of your life.

Online purchases are available or you can contact the author at

leepulpitman@sbcglobal.net

Made in the USA
Lexington, KY
14 February 2018